"Don't you see it?" he whispered harshly.

"Don't you know what's about to happen to you? You're on the verge of major success. It doesn't happen to many people, and I'd never try to take it from you."

I don't want major success, she thought, *I want you.* But she said, "You don't give me much credit, do you? You think I'll get so full of my own importance that I'll never come back to Ireland."

"No, that's not it at all... but I don't want to have you just on weekends, or every other month when you can sneak me a visit in between jobs. I want to be your life—or at least to share it all with you."

"That doesn't leave us with much, does it?" she asked weakly.

He mouthed a silent no. She nodded and let her numbed feet carry her out into the night.

Dear Reader,

Although our culture is always changing, the desire to love and be loved is a constant in every woman's heart. Silhouette Romances reflect that desire, sweeping you away with books that will make you laugh and cry, poignant stories that will move you time and time again.

This year we're featuring Romances with a playful twist. Remember those fun-loving heroines who always manage to get themselves into tricky predicaments? You'll enjoy reading about their escapades in Silhouette Romances by Brittany Young, Debbie Macomber, Annette Broadrick and Rita Rainville.

We're also publishing Romances by many of your all-time favorites such as Ginna Gray, Diana Palmer and Joan Hohl. Your overwhelming reaction to these authors has served as a touchstone for us, and we're pleased to bring you more books with Silhouette's distinctive medley of charm, wit and—above all—*romance*. I hope you enjoy this book, and the many stories to come.

Sincerely,

Rosalind Noonan
Senior Editor
SILHOUETTE BOOKS

LYNNETTE MORLAND
Irish Eyes

Silhouette Romance

Published by Silhouette Books New York

America's Publisher of Contemporary Romance

SILHOUETTE BOOKS
300 East 42nd St., New York, N.Y.   10017

Copyright © 1986 by Karen O'Connell

ISBN: 0-373-08432-3

First Silhouette Books printing May 1986

All the characters in this book are fictitious. Any
resemblance to actual persons, living or dead, is
purely coincidental.

America's Publisher of Contemporary Romance

Printed in the U.S.A.

Books by Lynnette Morland

Silhouette Romance

Occupational Hazard #339
Camera Shy #399
Irish Eyes #432

LYNNETTE MORLAND

lives in New York and considers it the most glorious city in the universe (although she plans to give London a chance to snatch the title). She loves antique clothing, drinking espresso in Greenwich Village cafés, reading in bed, and staying up all night to write her books.

ATLANTIC OCEAN

IRISH SEA

Ireland's Eye

Howth

Dublin

Dunquin

Dingle

Slea Head

CELTIC SEA

IRELAND

Chapter One

Robbie had never been stumped by a city yet. Of course she had never been in Europe before, but if twenty-two years in Manhattan had taught her any street sense, Dublin would be a cinch. She kept the map stuffed in her shoulder bag, wary now of pulling it out. It unfolded to the dimensions of a small tablecloth and acted as a flag of distress to passersby. In the few blocks from her hotel on O'Connell Street to the broad sweep of the River Liffey no fewer than four concerned souls had offered to help her find her way. They spoke in sweet, soft accents, not at all the heavy brogue of cartoon Irishmen and the genuineness of their concern delighted her.

She had spent the afternoon earnestly, if reluctantly, resting from the long flight. Her restless body had wanted to charge off in exploration; her common sense had forced it to relax. Fire Hazard's album would take two or three months to finish—plenty of time for her to explore. But tonight she had to meet the band and listen for the first time to their rehearsal. This left very little opportunity to recharge and become the sparkling American record producer they expected.

In the evening, after dozing in the darkened hotel room, she had slipped into fresh jeans, a sweatshirt and the jacket Michael had warned her to bring; (how would a New York City girl know to pack a jacket in August?) She checked her appearance in the mirror, not at all sure she looked her part. The image facing her looked rather plain compared to the glitzy reputation of people in rock music; but then she was one of the workhorses, she reminded herself, not one of the stars. Her black hair, as straight and shiny as unwoven silk, was blunt cut at her shoulders, her naturally honey-colored skin was innocent of all makeup save a bit of kohl stick that made her almond-shaped hazel eyes look even larger and more exotic. Her only two attributes that fit the rock norm were a natural slenderness and an abundance of leg.

Michael Shaw, the A & R man from Lawless Records, had met her in New York when he had first considered hiring her as Fire Hazard's producer. She must have passed muster since he had offered her the job; she wouldn't worry about it.

Eagerness to see this new city drove any lingering anxieties out of Robbie's mind as she set off through the busy streets. She scouted around for food she could take with her as a hospitable gesture to the band, and immediately saw three pizza parlors. Choosing one, she remarked to herself how much it resembled any pizza parlor she might find at home in Greenwich Village.

In fact, as Robbie wended her way down the wide, flower-decked boulevard, it occurred to her that Dublin as a whole looked disconcertingly American. The only visible difference was that the cars drove on the other side of the road. Robbie frowned in discomfort. Hadn't she been hired specifically because she specialized in a particular sound in rock music that people considered "American"? Fire Hazard had the same brash vigor of the other bands with which she had had success. Lawless Records had decided to hone that into a sound that would sell well in the big markets—Britain and the U.S. Enter Roberta Calderón.

She warned herself not to think about it that way. She was a *good* producer; she would help this young band make the best album they could, and if they happened to have great commercial success in the States, well, she wouldn't feel guilty about it.

Once over the river she wandered through a canyon of majestic old buildings that struck her as a bit more European than what she had seen so far. Michael's instructions sent her past them and into a waterside maze of tiny streets and alleys, which appeared to be a trendier neighborhood. A few punks sauntered comfortably along the cobbled streets, their pink and orange hairdos showing up alarmingly against the weathered paint on the little buildings.

Robbie found Crown Alley and looked around her in pleasure. Lights glowed from the shadows as neighborhood pubs warmed up for their evening business. At the end of the street the factory-style windows of a little café reflected the evening sun. A cup of coffee to wash down the pizza would be nice, she thought. As she headed toward the café she spied a little red sports car unattended at the curb in front of the rehearsal studio; its parking lights were on. In New York people locked up their cars so tightly, with shrieking burglar alarms and flashing lights, that the only person who could get into them was a thief, not a good Samaritan who wanted to save their battery for them. But this was a convertible. The chance to do a good deed without getting arrested for it pleased Robbie. She strolled over to shut off the lights.

This was easier said than done. An inveterate subway rider, Robbie had no great familiarity with cars, especially odd European models with the steering wheel on the right. She leaned into this one, poking tentatively along the steering column for the proper controls, and hoped she wouldn't hit the horn. No luck. Impatiently she climbed over the low door, sat down in the driver's seat and began a systematic survey of the dashboard. She felt ridiculous—she had apprenticed as a recording engineer at a thirty-two track studio, surely she could find one on/off switch.

In the midst of her concentration she felt the car sink. She looked up. There on the hood sat the most handsome man she had ever seen. That about summed it up—the absolute paragon of male beauty sat before her, relaxed as a lazing cougar, and the same sun-toasted color. The hot, silky energy that seemed to flow through his powerful body focused in his extraordinary eyes. They were deep-set and narrow—Eskimo eyes—as black and bright as volcanic glass. The short, bold strokes of his dark brows echoed the upsweep of his bronzed cheeks. Sprigs of sunny blond hair escaped from the darker mass that flowed in sweeping waves away from his face. Robbie's fingers felt an urge to smooth the errant strands back into place.

She nervously flexed those fingers in order to work the mischief out of them. He examined her with steady, sparkling interest and Robbie's usual aplomb fled. "Um . . . your lights were on. . . ." she explained.

"Ah."

"I know it looks like I'm stealing your car. . . ."

A smile curled into his attractive mouth, cutting creases into his cheeks. "No, it looks as if you're *failing* to steal my car."

Back came her sass; she rested her arms on the top of the teak steering wheel and assured him cheerfully, "Believe me, if I had wanted to steal your car, I could have hot-wired it in thirty seconds." In the interests of conversation she stretched the truth slightly.

His smile flashed out like a sudden flare of white sunshine and he laughed gaily. "So it's true then what we see on American television—all you Yanks are hooligans!"

"Yup. Either that or oil tycoons. And if I were the latter I'd have twelve of these cute little cars and *know* how to run the darn lights."

"Allow me to show you," he offered gallantly, and then, as he hopped off the fender and bent over the door, he paused and looked at her from the corner of one sharp eye. "For the time when you give up your thieving ways."

The muscular arm that invaded the small space between Robbie and the steering wheel passed so close to her breasts she shrank involuntarily into the soft leather seat. He noticed; she saw his jaw clench down a grin.

His disordered hair smelled fresh and cool, the tweedy green pullover he wore smelled wild and woodsy, spiced by an elusive hint of after-shave. She wanted to bury her nose in the wool and snuffle like a dog.

She resisted. Americans already had an odd-enough reputation abroad.

"There, now you'll know for the next time."

She had the presence of mind to glance up and notice which knob that he had twirled. Then, instead of withdrawing, he propped an elbow on the top of the windshield and cocked his sleek head. "Is there anything more you want to know?"

"About cars?" It popped out of her mouth so fast her common sense wasn't able to stop it. She struggled with a hot blush. He raised an eyebrow and stared at her frankly—but said nothing and made no move. Her words might have been a serious error in New York where men were more opportunistic. Here his courtesy gave her a chance to recover. "Thank you anyway, I'll have forgotten by the time I see the inside of a car again."

"Ah, that's a pity," he said with a sigh, straightening to his full height and stepping clear of the doorway. "I'm told I'm a fairly good teacher."

Robbie climbed quickly out of the car, accepting the aid of his arm as briefly as possible. The thought poked her that if he only taught automechanics he was going to waste, but she kept her mouth shut. Once on the curb with him she enjoyed the novel experience of feeling small. It wasn't his height and strapping build that impressed so much as his confident carriage. Though relaxed, one hip and one powerful leg carrying most of his weight, he looked collected and sure, equal to any scrutiny he might encounter. Robbie wondered what he did in life; she hoped he put all that great stage presence to use.

She herself stood five feet seven inches in her bare feet, which was rarely, since she habitually wore high-heeled boots to pull herself up a few extra inches. Women had a hard enough time in the rock world without looking small and inconsequential. Everything Robbie did was meant to add strength to her own impression of authority—her height, her no-nonsense uniform of a mannish jacket and plain jeans, the simple, stark haircut. Her look was forthright, her voice calm and strong. She had learned to freeze and outstare the hottest tempers and the rudest chauvinism in the business.

Beside this bold but polite and humorous Irishman she felt delicate and soft, yet not threatened or intimidated in any way. It was fortunate Simon hadn't been Irish. With the extra dose of charm he might have fooled her for considerably longer.

"Are you enjoying your holiday?" he inquired.

Robbie realized she had been drifting into old, troubled memories when she ought to be...to be...well, doing something worthy of this glorious man's attention. "It's gotten off to a great start." Good God, what if he took that wrong? What if he took it *right*? She hurried on, "Actually, I'm working while I'm here. But I plan to explore as much as I can—no sense wasting a chance to see a new country."

He seemed about to reply when a voice called from behind him, "Good evening to you!" He turned to acknowledge the call as Robbie dragged her attention to focus on the source. Entirely without her noticing a truck had pulled into Crown Alley and come to an idling halt behind the sports car. The man who spoke had jumped out of the cab to address them.

"Good evening," Robbie's blonde returned.

"Would you be moving your car any time in the near future? We're making a wee delivery."

Wee! Robbie had never before heard the word dropped in casual conversation. She had also never heard such a polite request from a truck driver in the middle of a city street. In New York he would have run up against the sports car's bumper and laid on the horn with earsplitting impatience.

"I will indeed," the black-eyed man promised. Then he cast Robbie a parting smile that sizzled the very blood in her veins. "I'm afraid this is goodbye, darlin'." He folded his long body into the impossibly small space of his car, saluted her with a wave and drove off.

Her gaze followed as his vehicle zipped around a corner and out of sight, then she reminded herself to back up along the sidewalk so the truck could pull in. She had a curiously dismal sense of loss that equally balanced the delight that remained from meeting such an attractive man. Some women—the brasher of her acquaintances—might have found a way to keep the encounter going, to have gotten his name or given him theirs, or whatever—in short, to have picked him up. Robbie couldn't do it. She supposed she was hopelessly backward, but she was stuck with herself.

As the driver and his assistant unlatched the side door of the truck, Robbie set her dreaming feet in motion toward the café. She still needed her coffee. What time was it in New York? Two in the afternoon...The flight and her nap had disoriented her.

A few minutes later, with the caffeine surging helpfully through her bloodstream, she made her way back up the street. She paused under the stone archway, balancing her heels on the bumpy cobbles. Already at twenty-two she was a veteran of her profession: five albums, countless singles and hints of a Grammy nomination under her belt. Why did she feel nervous all of a sudden, as if *this* album, *this* band brought her to a pivotal point in her career? She had come upon no significant evidence that Fire Hazard would change the future of rock, or even the future of Robbie Calderón. Only one thing could account for this feeling—jet lag.

Once within the tiny courtyard she could hear faint guitar chords filtering through the boarded-up third-story windows. A surge of pure enjoyment brought back her confidence.

Michael had said to go through the blue doors. Just able to drag one open, she energetically launched herself up the splintered, wooden steps. The place had the perfect ambience for a young, rough-edged band—it was dark, derelict and banged up by years of hard use.

The second-floor landing led off into seemingly unused warehouse space, the third floor improved on that by looking just as bleak, but tinkling with the sound of young laughter and guitar notes. Robbie braved the doorway and came upon a familiar scene. Young men, barely out of their teens, lounged with cigarettes and guitars; girls perched alongside them, lending color and moral support. The focus seemed to be a small, army-booted girl who stood in the center of a cleared space tapping her blue-polished fingernails against a microphone. Her white-blond hair was cut so close to her head that it stood up like a brush, setting off her black-lined eyes and high cheek-boned, pixie face. This must be the singer, Mairead Lalor, Robbie decided. Michael had helped her find a way to remember the unfamiliar first name by pointing out that it rhymed with "parade."

In a quick survey, she located the other band members and identified them by their instruments—Micky Hennessey on drums, Sean Cronin bass, Eamonn McInnes lead guitar, which left rhythm guitar and voice to Mairead. They were a presentable-looking bunch—

young, scruffy and stylishly decked out in thrift-shop chic.

Stepping into the light, Robbie announced her presence. "Somebody here order a pizza from New York?"

Heads swiveled and Mairead's face glowed with a vivacious smile that showed one charmingly crooked tooth. "You don't look at all like a pizza."

Robbie laughed and felt with relief that they would get along. She strode comfortably into the midst of her new clients and delighted them by correctly naming each. Mairead was the most voluble, a tiny scrap of a girl with enough rapid-fire chatter to make up for the more retiring of her bandmates. In talk Eamonn, a classic Irish redhead, came in a close second. Their competing lines of commentary overlapped in a bewildering tangle. Robbie's head whirled after a few short minutes of sorting them out.

Sean hid shyly behind a fall of thick, dark bangs, smiling sweetly, but utterly silent. Micky darted around the knot of people and handed Robbie a beer. He seemed to be the most calm, efficient one, she decided, neither a chatter-box like Eamonn or Mairead, nor a recluse like Sean.

Breaking the ice accomplished, it remained for Robbie to get their attention onto the music without making them self-conscious. At one point in the introductory chat, she picked up Eamonn's shocking-orange guitar, chosen to complement his hair, no doubt, and plucked a few strings. She played well enough to produce tunes and badly enough to make real musicians snatch their instruments out of her hands and show her how one *really* played.

"I heard some pretty little song while I was checking into my hotel today. Let me see if I can remember any of it." She strummed. They concentrated fiercely. She strummed some more. At their still-perplexed faces she resorted to humming.

"Oh yeah!" Eamonn brightened, quite a feat with his already fluorescent coloring. "'The Rising of the Moon'—it's an old rebel song."

Mairead jumped in. "It's usually done a wee bit faster though, to get the blood up. What hotel are you stuck in?"

"The Gresham."

The tiny blonde rolled her eyes. "Ach well—they wouldn't want to ruffle the feathers of the Aga Khan. You're not *really* staying there, are you?"

"The record company made the arrangements," Robbie explained.

"I suppose you're used to a cush place then anyway, being from New York."

"Hardly!" Robbie laughed. "I was raised on the Lower East Side of Manhattan with Puerto Rican immigrants on one end of the block and Hell's Angels on the other. The closest I ever got to a hotel before the age of eighteen was passing the flophouses along the Bowery on my way to school." Though these scrub-faced Irish kids couldn't appreciate the specifics of her childhood environment, they were familiar enough with the key names like the Bowery and the Lower East Side to get a general idea.

"Your name then—Calderón—is it Puerto Rican?"

"No, Spanish. My grandfather came from Madrid. I got nothing but the name and the coloring. I don't even speak Spanish except for what I learned from the kids on the street." She grimaced. "And none of it is exactly polite."

Eamonn cracked another grin at her. "We'll send you back to New York with a good dose of Finglas slang then."

"What's 'Finglas'?"

"It's Dublin's version of the Lower East Side."

"Lots of squatters and kids on gur," Mairead added.

Robbie looked so mystified Micky was inspired to throw his own explanation into the discussion. "'On gur' means having no place to live. They also call it 'sleeping rough.'"

"At least I know what 'squatters' are. There are a lot of people without homes in Dublin?" Somehow Robbie hadn't thought quaint little Irish cities would be vulnerable to hard-core urban problems.

"Lots," Micky assured her, almost jovially. "Kids especially—runaways, kids that get thrown out."

"They're our biggest fans. They sneak into all our gigs." Mairead chuckled. "And you know that when this record of ours comes out they'll be sure to steal it from the shops."

Robbie thought they took all this very lightly. Then again, it was hardly her place to come off like a social worker. What did she know of their *own* backgrounds? Did they come from nice homes or would they straggle out to some Finglas squat when they left the rehearsal studio that night? She hoped the record company had given them a reasonable advance on the album....

This reminded her that she *did* have to coax a little music out of them if the thing was ever going to get made. She opted for the direct approach. "Well, let's give them something worth ripping off then." She handed the guitar back to Eamonn and said severely, "Play!"

After one short moment of nervousness, Fire Hazard threw themselves into action. Sean's bass set up a line of rhythm that reverberated through the decaying wooden floor. Micky leaped to his drum kit and pumped up the beat. Mairead whooped and clapped even before her time came to sing, complementing Eamonn's guitar playing much more sympathetically than she had his talk.

Robbie covertly pulled out her stopwatch and started her first rough timing of the selection. She smiled to herself; as their leadoff song they had wisely chosen a real rouser. This sort of sense would serve them well in concert. It was the producer's job to represent them just as well on vinyl.

After an hour they had crashed enthusiastically through a dozen original songs, and Robbie's little notebook was filled with notes on instrumentation and potential problems. She called a break even though the spirit of fun was holding firm. She could hear Mairead's voice begin to tear on the high notes, and Micky's drumming had lost some of its precision. They were pushing themselves in order to make a good impression on her. They *had*. They were so eager and open-minded, so unlike the bored, pompous musicians she had sometimes worked with. She liked eagerness, even if worldlier heads would call it naïveté. She supposed that in a lot of ways she was quite naive herself.

"I don't know what kind of labor laws you've got over here, but in the U.S. it's illegal to make a producer work past ten o'clock without food. And that pizza doesn't count—Eamonn ate five pieces."

Eamonn cast her a pitying look. "That's the problem with you Yanks—you're soft. But," and here he sighed in apparent resignation, "in the name of good foreign relations I suppose we can force ourselves to take a drop of tea with you.''

Before Robbie could thrust her arms through the sleeves of her jacket the band had laid their instruments aside and started to run for the door. ''Hey!'' she yelled to get their attention. ''Where are we going?''

''Oh there's a wee pub around the corner—they don't know us there yet, so they won't bolt the doors shut when they see us coming.''

Mairead giggled. ''They'll learn, though. By the end of this album we'll be scrounging for pints way up in Ballymun!''

Robbie made a mental note to find out how far away this Ballymun might be. Then she dashed after her band.

The pub satisfied Robbie's desire for local color. It was a tiny little place, dark with an ornate, black-stained oak bar and open booths called snugs. There were no private tables; the patrons either piled onto available benches, sending up clouds of tobacco smoke from the upholstery, or dragged over whatever little stools could be found in corners. As at any bar, conversation proceeded at the top of the lungs, with much sign language. Fortunately Robbie felt comfortable enough with her new clients to just settle back and let the tension of the trip and prerehearsal jitters trickle away.

Mairead squeezed in next to her and pumped her with questions while they wolfed down sandwiches and pints of warm, bitter Guinness. Was Robbie married? Did she have a sweetheart? Had she ever met so-and-so from such and such a band? What were the clubs like in New York? The clubs in Dublin were a dead loss, the singer informed her with a disgusted pout, nothing but teenagers and the old bores who were trying to act young.

Robbie assured her that it was much the same in New York, but the girl looked disappointed. Then Robbie managed to dredge up one tale of a party that had somewhat escaped the normal bounds. In fact, it had turned into a two-year-long lawsuit with the apartment building's owners. Prodded on by Mairead's questions, she also told her about the sessions with one singer who had been so strung out on drugs that her private doctor had to be present for every hair-raising minute. Neither of these events had been fun or uplifting at the time, as much of the rock world failed to uplift Robbie, but they seemed to be the kind of stories Mairead was eager to hear.

Mairead's green eyes lit up like emeralds and she leaned in confidentially to Robbie's ear. "Me brother would *die* to hear you talk!"

"Why?"

"You'd think he was some toothless old granda the way he goes on about me and my friends. He thinks I'm too wild by half. As if he wasn't *worse* when he was my age!" She went on, obviously launched into a favorite complaint. "You can't bring it up but he says, 'I made those mistakes. I won't have you making them all over for yourself.' You'd think I was one step away from the abyss of hell to watch him glare."

Robbie could see Mairead's point, one had to make one's own mistakes in life or the lessons would not stick half so well. But on the other hand, she felt a fleeting envy for Mairead that she *had* a brother who cared enough to worry and criticize. She herself had been the only child of a timid couple who worked sixteen hours a day to keep their little store going in a neighborhood decayed by poverty and crime. They had loved her, but in a tired, sad way. Whatever trouble she had strayed into as a youngster, and there had been some, she had extricated herself from it with her own wit and common sense.

A soft poke in her side roused her. Mairead said tenderly, "You're looking thoughtful. Has this talk of me brother depressed you?"

"Oh no, of course not. I guess it's just the plane ride catching up to me."

"Well, sure, that's it. It's criminal us keeping you up like this. Mick! Sean! Where's Eamonn? Well, drag him off the dart game then! We're killing this poor foreigner with our low ways. Come on, have the barman call her a taxi."

"What?" Robbie protested. "We've only gone through half your songs...."

Mairead looked at her kindly, her gaze much older than her rosy face. "We've all the time in the world. Are you in such a hurry to leave Ireland?"

Chapter Two

Robbie bounded out of bed the next morning, grateful for the vigorous constitution that helped her get herself out of the room in time for the shy young maids to clean it. Now that the initial thrill was past, she decided that she disliked living in a hotel, particularly one that seemed to cater to people who owned furs and matching luggage. Perhaps she could rent a little house somewhere.... She'd have to ask Michael. As the liaison between Lawless and Fire Hazard, which in a way now included Robbie, he might take care of such arrangements.

She treated herself to a breakfast of coffee and something called a "fry," which proved to be exactly that—fried sausages, fried ham, fried eggs and, most delicious of all, fried slabs of Irish soda bread. How did people here stay thin? She hadn't seen one yet who could be rightly called fat, though some men boasted slight beer bellies.

When she returned to the Gresham the desk clerk scurried across the blue-carpeted lobby to give her a message. Mairead had called and left a number where she could be reached. Back in her meticulously tidied room, Robbie sat down and placed the call, wondering if the unfamiliar sounds on the line were rings or a busy signal. Mairead's throaty "Hullo?" answered her.

"Ah, Robbie, out exploring already, were you?"

"I didn't get too far, just down the block for breakfast."

"What? No breakfast in bed? What good is staying in a posh hotel?"

"No good at all for me, I'm afraid. I'm just a peasant at heart. I don't suppose there are apartments or houses available for as short a time as I'm going to be here, are there?"

"Sure there are, though the rent would be dear.... I forgot—Lawless is paying for it, aren't they? God knows the *Gresham* can't be cheap." Her meditative tone firmed up with sudden decision. "I'll nip out and get the morning paper. We'll have you settled somewhere cozy in two shakes—somewhere you can make a drop of tea for yourself without sending the kitchen staff into a tizzy. You can come out here and we'll go over the ads and make some calls."

"But where *are* you, Mairead?"

"Oh, I'm at my brother's. I've got a key and I sleep in the spare room when it's too late to trouble going all the way back to Howth."

"Where's Howth?"

"It's up the coast, north of Dublin. A suburb you'd call it. I'm the last one at home—my sister, Rose, just married last summer and of course my brother Christy's been on his own for years."

So Mairead, for all her punkish haircut and bold behavior, still lived in her parents' house. Robbie liked that. She also found it sweet that, aggrieved by her brother as Mairead pretended to be, she still felt quite free to bed down in his house . . . the whereabouts of which remained a mystery.

"So how do I get to your brother's house?"

"Do you want to take a taxi or the bus?"

"I feel adventurous—the bus."

Mairead gave her instructions and promised to have "real American-style coffee" waiting for her when she got there. Wondering what "real American-style coffee" could be, Robbie checked to make sure the map was still in her bag and set off once more.

The bus took her through gorgeous residential sections with tree-lined streets and stately homes. The conductor read the address Robbie had written on a slip of paper and, to her surprise, made sure she got off at the right stop on Northumberland Road. What conductor in New York would do that, she wondered. For that matter, what bus in New York would *have* a conductor?

Tucking her jacket more tightly against the damp breeze, Robbie surveyed the house. It was a lovely, red-brick Georgian ornamented with white stonework and black iron. The yard was a healthy tangle of hedges, ivy and fragrant mint that grew between the stones of the slate walk. At the top of worn marble steps stood a shiny red door set with a brass knob, a lion-headed knocker and a nameplate that read "O'Laighleis." How did one pronounce such a combination of letters? she wondered. And was it Irish for Mairead's last name of Lalor or something else?

She shrugged off her questions and thumped the ring in the lion's mouth.

"Come in! Come in!" Mairead greeted in her sing-song manner. "I've just put the kettle on to boil."

This morning Fire Hazard's singer had on a fairly conservative outfit—jeans and a fiery yellow, oversize sweatshirt printed with the seal of Trinity College.

"Why, Mairead, I had no idea you were a scholar as well as a singer," Robbie teased.

"Ach! To be sure it's Christy's. I have to raid his wardrobe when I spend the odd night. Thank God he still has some decent duds left from normal life or else you'd find me in trousers and tweed jackets. I don't know how he stands it—he used to have such sharp taste."

"What exactly does he *do*?" Robbie was building up a portrait of a Christy O'Laighleis who puttered around the musty, ivy-laden halls of Trinity College, perhaps with his teeth clamped on the stem of a pipe and his critical eyes glowering from behind a pair of specta-cles. She had a conflicting suspicion that any profes-sion so stiff and academic would be unable to support a life-style that included a Georgian house in this part of town.

Mairead had spent a second or two looking per-plexed. "The fearful thing is that I don't exactly know. He finished up a degree at Trinity a couple of years ago in a subject he pretty much made up himself—Adoles-cent Sociology and Mass Media, or some foolish title. Now he's a consultant to the government setting up new radio programming for the 'younger audience.' So you see," she continued with a mischievous smile, "I'm terribly well connected." Then her look changed to one of anxiety. "That's not how we got the recording contract though! No one at Lawless knew I was related to Christy at all, although I suppose they do now."

"Well, your names are so different—unless Lalor is just the English for O'Luh...O'Lah..." She stumbled over the foreign name.

Mairead giggled and replied, "No, it's a different name all together. I didn't want anyone to think I was living off my brother's influence."

From what she had heard of brother Christy's opinions on rock, Robbie thought it unlikely he'd pull strings to advance his sister's career, but it seemed less important to mention this than to reassure the young singer. "No one would think that after hearing your music, believe me. You can go as far as you want in the business, Mairead. I've heard a lot of bands and yours has got it, whatever the hell 'it' is."

The blonde ducked her head to hide an ear-to-ear grin. "Well, let's go see if I can manage coffee. If you're wrong about the band I may need a skill to fall back on."

The house surprised Robbie. Its interior had been designed for a formal, wealthy way of life—high ceilings, chandeliers, elaborately carved moldings—but it had been redone for a modern man of subtle, ascetic taste. The furniture was sparse and simple, though comfortable, the colors subdued. The only ornaments were a few simple, lovely paintings and small bits of sculpture. The place had an immediately calming effect; it would have been a soothing refuge from the chaos of city life, even New York city life.

Mairead took Robbie downstairs into the fresh blue-and-white kitchen. "Mairead, this kitchen is big enough to rent out as a separate apartment. Is your brother a gourmet cook or something?''

"Oh, he can manage for himself when he must, but that's about it.''

"He's not married then?" Robbie hoped the question didn't sound too inquisitive.

Mairead took no special notice. "No, to my parents' great grief. Thirty-five and as stubborn a bachelor as you're likely to see.''

"Why is that?" Robbie moved to hold the coffee makings as the younger girl climbed bodily onto the counter top.

"I have two theories on it—maybe it's a bit of both of them. Number one, I think he has a low opinion of most women. You see, making allowances for my own prejudice, he's as handsome as the devil himself. He's been shaking the females off of his ankles since before his beard came in. I suppose it's a *crippling* disability.''

She stated this in such a scathing manner Robbie burst out laughing. "You and your brother must be like fire and tinder together.''

"We are at that," Mairead said, grinning. "Though each on our own is as mild as milk.''

Robbie couldn't imagine this lively girl ever being so bland. "What's your second theory?''

"That he's afraid. He never does anything by halves; he throws himself body and soul into whatever has a grip on his heart and, consequently, he gets his heart broken.''

"Oh..." Robbie mused, thinking of Simon. "He's had a bad romance or two?''

"Well, no, not exactly. You see, he's such a passionate person and he's been involved in *projects* that have broken his heart. He practically has a target painted on his chest. He's so idealistic that when he finally finds a woman who meets his expectations he's going to fall *hard*. He's survived the business catastrophes, but he's terrified that he won't survive what a woman could do to him.''

"With age comes wisdom," Robbie muttered in sympathy.

The coffee-making operation left Robbie's hostess quite exhausted, unfamiliar as she was with any cooking process that didn't involve frying. Robbie kept silent throughout. Instant coffee would have suited her perfectly, but such a substance was nowhere to be found in the house of Christy O'Laighleis. Was Mairead's brother as passionate and obsessive about coffee as he was about everything else?

Upstairs, draped over the huge, upholstered cushions of the low couches, they enjoyed the results of Mairead's labor and scoured the morning papers.

"It's criminal what they're asking for flats!" Mairead gasped at every ad. Robbie translated the rents into dollars and privately thought the cost quite reasonable. She would have paid much more for the privilege of living in a real house and riding to work each day on buses where the passengers treated her as an adopted cousin. For that matter, she could *walk* into town from a neighborhood as close as this, and the walk would take her through very beautiful streets.

Full of enthusiasm and an inexplicable sense of responsibility for her American producer, Mairead set about calling landlords and crossing off ads in a most efficient manner. Too efficient—in a matter of an hour she had reduced the possibilities to three and made appointments to see them the following day. She grumbled after hanging up for the final time, "You've got to know the prime minister to get a decent place anymore."

Robbie couldn't resist. "I thought you said you were well connected with the government. Isn't the prime minister a personal friend of your brother's?"

Mairead considered that remark much too seriously. "I wonder if Christy *can* help...."

"Oh, no! I didn't mean..."

"Ach, don't worry—he won't be getting any special laws passed for you or anything. What I was thinking is a lot less exciting than that—just that he's gossiped over the fence with enough of the old biddies on the street that he might catch word of something coming up. I'll hit him tonight at supper. Will you stay? I've a fair hand with a fry."

Robbie declined reluctantly; she had become curious to meet this odd brother, but she had already planned to spend the afternoon at the recording studio getting to know the engineer who would be working with her on Fire Hazard's album. She had also decided, for the sake of what figure she had, to stay away from fries.

Mairead sighed and added provocatively, "I guess Christy will just have to wait a bit longer to see that you don't have the mark of the fiend on you."

"Why does he think that? He doesn't *know* me!"

"You've got to remember that he's down on this whole rock and roll business. And I suppose he wasn't too keen on those stories of yours."

Mairead had told her starchy brother the stories Robbie had recounted at the pub? No wonder he had been unfavorably impressed. The girl must have an insatiable desire to incite.

"When did you see him long enough to singe his ear off like that?"

"When he got home late last night from his date."

"I thought you said he didn't like women."

"I didn't say he was dead!"

Regardless of whatever Mairead's fearful brother thought of her, Robbie spent the afternoon in a most serious and unshocking manner. The studio that had been engaged for Fire Hazard's recording sessions lay at the end of another alley—a true alley this time rather than a street. Just around the corner rose the stern, soot-streaked edifices of Ireland's government and its great cultural institutions.

She liked the fact that the city was too small to segregate its state offices from the scruffier of its enterprises. In the United States people were scandalized to one degree or another when the name of a politician became linked to that of a rock star. Robbie had always resented this fact—she was positive that politics would benefit from a dose of music.

In a very good humor she introduced herself at the studio door and was allowed into the control booth of the room she'd be using. Carefully keeping herself to the background, she observed the session in progress. The receptionist had told her it was a demo for a young folk singer and that the head engineer, Donal Sheehy, was producing it himself, with "help" from the girl's manager.

Robbie noted approvingly how calm Donal remained as the manager jabbered questions and suggestions in his ear, and how his easy confidence transmitted itself across the glass to the nervous, redheaded singer. Robbie tended to the easygoing end of the spectrum herself. Even Simon had concealed his nervous excitability with an apparent relaxation in the studio. Stars could afford to be hysterical, producers could not.

Within half an hour she had seen enough of Donal's deft touch with music and people to know he'd be easy to work with. She itched to dive into actual recording, even though she had heard only one Fire Hazard rehearsal. It was too early to plan specifics with him, but they *could* discuss a general approach and he could explain the unique abilities of Emerald Studios' facilities and staff.

Over dinner at one of the neighborhood pubs Donal hoisted a pint of ale at her. "I must say, it'll be a rare pleasure working with someone who understands the nuts and bolts of the job. How does a wee girleen like yourself come by so much knowledge?"

His automatic male prejudice was standard in the industry. She let it slip by without comment, preferring to prove by action rather than by argument that women could handle any job in music they chose. "I spent six months as an apprentice engineer in New York—that was *after* another half year hanging around the studio fetching coffee. I watched and listened, I sent to manufacturers for the equipment specifications and studied them, I read technical magazines.... Actually, it was pretty easy for me. I like machines—they make more sense than people sometimes."

"They do indeed!" He threw back his graying head and laughed. "Well, you have the knack, there's no doubt. Tell me, why didn't you stick with it? How did you get sidetracked into producing?"

Along with a certain degree of chauvinism, another attitude that seemed international was the high regard of engineers for their craft. They saw themselves as the sane professionals who actually turned out the music, whereas producers were troublemakers or madmen, nearly as irrational as the artists. Sharing a good deal of this prejudice, Robbie gave him an ironic smile, "Ah, same old story—it was a man...."

He nodded knowingly, then asked in a dark voice, "Simon Beyer?"

Startled, Robbie replied, "Gossip really spreads in this business doesn't it?"

"We're not quite *so* far off the beaten path here, you know. Every few years or so a shipwrecked sailor brings news from the outside world."

"I'm sorry, Donal. I didn't mean it as a put-down. In fact, I *like* the fact that Ireland isn't right plunk in the middle of the rock and roll circus. It's a rest from some of the nonsense I have to put up with in New York and Los Angeles. People think it's so glamorous and it must be so much fun.... Argh!" Her eyes nearly crossed in frustration—it wasn't even just starstruck fans who thought this; her own friends were so happily caught up in the party scene that she never even bothered to voice a complaint. They would have looked at her blankly.

"Aye, it's a crazy business.... Your Simon Beyer was quite a trend-maker for a few years there. And where is he now?"

"Exactly. The market fell out of the particular sound he was into. He's talented, but he won't produce jazz or classical or anything that isn't superpopular."

"Sounds like you still have a bit of a soft spot for him."

Robbie shook her head, "I'm grateful, that's all. He originally made me his assistant in order to have me around for company, but as soon as he saw that I was more than ornamental, he let me prove myself. You can hardly be indifferent to someone who opens the door out of pure generosity.''

''Was it out of that, I wonder?''

Robbie frowned at the half-mumbled remark.

Donal's shrewd glance flickered over her, but he continued anyway, ''Somehow I thought there was a romance.''

''There was,'' she admitted quietly. ''But that came later. For nearly three years it was strictly business.''

''Ach! I surrender! I don't even know the fellow, except by hearsay, so I'll yield to your judgment. A toast to Simon Beyer—may he continue to recognize gold whenever he stumbles upon it.''

''May we all!'' Robbie endorsed heartily, bumping her glass to his. ''How do you say 'health' in Irish? Slainte!''

Donal, as had Fire Hazard the night before him, seemed to have a vastly greater capacity for drink than Robbie. She excused herself and left the pub long before she reached what she considered her limit of safety, but out on the sidewalk she was appalled to find herself woozy. The whole walk from Roger's Lane to Crown Alley passed in a blur of trees and small shops.

In front of the rehearsal studio, she found her glance skipping over the parked cars and realized she had half hoped to see a little red one. She had arrived at roughly the same time the previous day—the sun had skimmed the slate roofs at the same angle. If the black-eyed man worked in the neighborhood it was just possible that . . . but no. Surprised at the cloud of disappointment that dropped into her spirits, Robbie headed for the doorway.

Only the boys met her upstairs. Their assorted friends and moral supporters were absent, which Robbie took as a sign that the band now felt comfortable with her and would settle into serious work patterns. But Mairead was late. Robbie suffered a momentary qualm; she hoped fervently that no one in this delightful band would turn out to be irresponsible, especially not Mairead, whom she had already come to like so well.

"Have you heard from her?" she inquired.

No one seemed concerned. "She's a good girl, she'll be along."

So Robbie forced herself to put the worry out of her mind. Instead she started to draw a diagram of Micky's drum kit so Donal could plan how to mike it.

Creaks from the rickety stairs and the sound of Mairead's distinctive voice caught Robbie's attention a few minutes later. The girl seemed to be making a point, in testy irritation, to a companion. Robbie looked up from her crouch on the far side of the loft. Mairead stomped into the room wearing the same yellow sweatshirt, and talking over her shoulder to...the owner of the red sports car. Christy! Robbie's heart gave a lurch.

He looked no less dazzling than she remembered. The casual sweater and slacks of the evening before had given way to a suit of cream-colored linen. The fabric was just crisp enough to look neat, yet slouchy enough to flow with his long, lazy grace, and the soft color made his skin and hair glow a toasted gold. How did one get tan in Ireland? The dressiness of his outfit suggested that he had another date lined up. Robbie swallowed hard and envied the woman. She hesitated between hiding behind the amp and boldly standing up. The bold approach won.

Her sudden movement caught Christy's eye, while Mairead wrangled on. A crescent-shaped smile dug into one burnt brown cheek, but there was something wrong. The smile didn't reach his eyes or touch them with the humor she had seen before. Robbie steeled herself—he was no longer simply a gorgeous man, he was a brother who disapproved of his sister's life-style, who had heard two of Robbie's most infamous stories and who probably, even allowing for Mairead's tendency to exaggerate, wondered now how bad an influence she might be. As soon as he had a few moments to get to know her, Robbie knew his worry would clear. She was no wild-eyed rocker by any stretch of the imagination.

"Ah, Robbie, there you are now." Mairead cut her harangue short. "I've brought Christy up so he could meet you and tell all the dithering old fussbudgets on the street what a dear, sweet thing you are and what a grand tenant you'd make."

Unmoved by Mairead's extravagance, to which he was probably inured, Christy O'Laighleis extended his powerful, long-fingered hand and caught Robbie's in a grip just hard enough to hint at a threat. She saw dark speculation in his glittering eyes and knew she had to head him off at the pass. "Did you remember to turn off your lights this time?"

"I did," he replied equably. "God forbid I should tempt the tourists."

"Huh?" Mairead's quizzical look reminded Robbie that, tempted as she was to forget the existence of everyone else in the room, this was not a private conversation. Why couldn't Mairead's brother be a bit less incredibly attractive?

"Your brother and I sort of met last night. It looked as if I was trying to steal his car."

Mairead's consternation was rendered total when Christy added, "The circumstances were a bit misleading, but I always try to delve beneath appearances."

"An admirable trait," Robbie agreed significantly.

"Yes, I soon discovered that she hadn't the faintest idea how to steal a car. We came up with another explanation..."

Mairead shook her head. "The two of you are jabbering nonsense. Is this how you handle the deputies in Parliament, Christy?"

"They hardly need my help to be confused. Politicians are naturally muddled."

"If they are so hopeless, why do you work with them?" Robbie asked.

"Oh, no one is *hopeless*. At least I'm romantic enough to kid myself that they aren't."

Mairead whistled in skepticism. "That's the biggest crock I've ever heard, Christy. You're a card-carrying cynic, is what you are, and you've no business standing here with the glower on your face, depressing everyone."

Robbie thought he quite lit up the room, glower or no glower, but she allowed that a sister's viewpoint might differ. He feigned such hurt surprise Robbie had to laugh. Even Mairead grumbled, unable to maintain her annoyance.

Eamonn, who had been uncharacteristically silent, swung his guitar strap over his head and reminded them gruffly, "I don't suppose you could fit a few notes of rehearsal into this domestic drama, could you now, Mairead?"

After she had thrown a wad of paper at him, the singer turned archly to her brother and began, "Well..."

With wry humor he clasped her shoulders in his big hands and said earnestly, "Sister, darling, I'd stay to give you the benefit of my criticism but..."

"But Helena's waiting."

"Not Helena—Aideen."

Mairead made big eyes. "Oh, you *can* tell all your women apart!"

He gave her a playful swat and turned on his booted heel. "Oh, you know we've left the dinner in the car."

"Oh, blessed saints, so we have. I'll just pop down with you and get it...."

He forestalled her. "Shouldn't you be warming up or something professional like that? Ms. Calderón can come down."

"Aren't *you* the bossy..."

"No, he's right, Mairead. I'm not needed right now and you are." Robbie knew beyond question that Christy had made the suggestion in order to have a word with her. There would be no use evading him; perhaps one rational, friendly little talk would clear up his suspicions. They didn't seem to have evaporated as quickly as they should have.

She preceded him into the stairwell, so intensely aware of his eyes on the back of her neck that she nearly missed the top steps. Unnerved further by the grip that clamped onto her arm and hauled her back into balance, she cast about for a light remark. "That's the trouble with young, unknown bands—they get these dangerous places to practice in. As soon as Fire Hazard is famous they'll be setting up in Dublin Castle itself."

She saw by the grim set of his mouth that he was not amused. This was going to be hard. Thoughtful, she kept her silence until they reached the tiny courtyard. He still hadn't said anything to her, perhaps he wasn't going to. Perhaps his disapproval was not as terrible as her own and Mairead's imagination would have it. She shrugged mentally and passed through the archway. Only then did she hear the ominous timbre of his voice. "Ms. Calderón."

Of course he had waited until they were beyond the sound-carrying shaft of the courtyard. She swung around, hiding an involuntary shiver, even as she remarked pleasantly, "*Robbie*, please."

"Ms. Calderón," he repeated, eyes like cold onyx. "A friendly warning..."

"How friendly?" she asked drily, just to see his lips tighten.

"Perhaps friendlier than I feel." He closed in, hands thrust safely into the pockets of his trousers, but his leonine body was charged with an aggressive tension that belied the casual pose. "The truth is this—you and I can spar as we like and it's only good fun. But my sister is a different story. She talks a grand line but underneath the clothes and the hair she's young and naive, *impressionable*."

"She strikes me as a very strong young lady."

"Oh indeed. I believe the word is 'headstrong.' She doesn't need someone stuffing nonsense between her ears—she's quite capable of it herself."

Robbie allowed herself the luxury of an annoyed look. It bounced off him like a ball off the side of a house, he was that moved. Her height and her practiced, intimidating manner had no effect on him. "I take it *I'm* the one stuffing in the nonsense. Having known her for all of twenty-four hours, I've corrupted her beyond redemption...."

His handsome, thunder-filled face loomed suddenly within inches of hers and extinguished her taste for sarcasm. "We're not so backward here that we don't know a thing or two about the world. England is right on our doorstep and the airwaves are filled with American music and television. Every kid uses slang that fits the Detroit ghetto better than it does some little fishing village on the coast of Mayo. We've actually got a heroin epidemic here in Dublin now, with signs of another in Cork."

As she put her speech of protest together in her mind, he seemed to remember the alleged purpose of the trip and lifted a cooler from the well behind the car seats. When he swung it her way she automatically extended her arms. She hadn't realized, from the easy way he handled it, that its weight would wrench the breath right out of her. She hung on grimly, her comment freshly inspired by this annoyance. "Gee, I had no idea my evil plan for Ireland's destruction would start to work so quickly."

"You take it lightly."

"I do not, but I allow myself a chuckle to think that the Irish Parliament has nothing more pressing to do than discuss *my* reputation. Or is it the radio people who are worried?"

For the briefest moment she thought she saw humor flicker through his face, but maybe it was only the light glinting off his eyes. His next utterance was grim. "Neither, in fact—although there are a few special names that raise hackles in the circles of Irish radio— and Simon Beyer is one of them."

"I'll let him know that if and when I ever see him again."

He continued as if he hadn't heard her. "Now your past is your past and I've made a raft of mistakes myself—things I'd consider mistakes now—but my sister doesn't need to repeat them. With your cooperation she won't—if you take my meaning."

Robbie braced herself to be severe. "You know, Mairead is not exactly *dabbling* in rock. She's got a recording contract with a company that believes in her. She's got a *producer* who believes in her. She's *already* neck deep in this wicked world."

"Just don't *you* be the one to push her head under, Ms. Calderón. While you're here you're on your best behavior, shall we agree to that? Whatever habits you've picked up from people like Simon Beyer you left behind you at customs—don't go spinning her tales of how glamorous it is to be a highly paid, drugged-up waste of life. Do I make myself understood?"

"You make it very tempting for me to show Mairead what other life-styles are available, just so she doesn't think you are God's voice on earth."

He very blatantly used all his height and mass to cast a heavy shadow over her in the darkening alley. To her own dismay, she shivered.

"Ms. Calderón, I hope you will *resist* the temptation."

Christy did not watch Robbie storm back into the warehouse, he was too annoyed—inexplicably so. Sliding behind the wheel of his car he recalled vividly events just twenty-four hours old that had occurred on this very street and given him such unexpected pleasure. The image of that lovely American girl, frowning so charmingly at the dashboard of his car, had buoyed him through his evening. Anything that could keep his spirits afloat through a formal dinner with a dreary assistant cabinet minister had to have caught hold of his imagination quite firmly.

During the bureaucrat's nasal chitchat, and the inane comments of his own lady companion, Christy had found his thoughts dwelling pleasantly on the American's delicate, creamy face, the rosy lips parted in a smile that was open and warm, but not brash. He hated the trend toward boldness—no, toward outright ill grace—that he had noted among Irish girls. While he hardly wanted to see a woman who was meek and wishy-washy, he appreciated one who managed to balance self-confidence with a bit of grace.

This American exhibited all his favorite traits—wit, assurance, quiet style—and, if that wasn't enough, she was stunning. It had briefly crossed his mind to wonder whether there was a connection between her and the producer who had been scheduled to show up at Mairead's rehearsal, but he had dismissed the possibility after hearing Mairead parrot those offensive anecdotes. The young woman who had tried to save his battery could not be the source of such stories.

Which just went to prove how trustworthy his heart was on the subject of women. He should let his *head* deal with the fair sex, he reminded himself, as he had done successfully for years. Grinding his teeth, he put the little car in gear and screeched through Crown Alley toward his date with . . . who was it again? Aideen.

Chapter Three

When Robbie came back upstairs she was alone and mad. She let the cooler drop with a slam that caused her band to wince collectively.

"Ah, there goes the pheasant under glass," Eamonn mourned.

"Sorry."

"Nah," Mairead supplied. "It's just sausage sandwiches. Take more than a ham-handed American to bruise them."

Robbie knew Mairead meant nothing hurtful by the jest, but her nerves had just been sandpapered by Mairead's brother. "Better ham-handed than mutton-headed," she mumbled sourly. "Okay, the party's over, gang. Is this a band or a social club?"

Surprised, they scrambled for their instruments. Robbie determinedly plopped herself on a bench, notebook and stopwatch in hand, and nodded for Mairead to count the beat.

Half a song sufficed to cool Robbie's temper. Disapproving relatives were no novelty in rock, she just rarely encountered them in person. And, to be honest, had Christy O'Laighleis been less attractive, she would have reassured him and forgotten the incident. *She* knew she was no danger to Mairead. The girl was set on a career in rock; nothing short of brain surgery would discourage her. Viewed from that point, she was darn lucky to have someone as businesslike and, Robbie almost chuckled as the word came into her mind, *wholesome* as Roberta Calderón to produce her first record. Plenty of sharks roamed the waters, cruising for fresh blood, hungry to exploit kids who didn't know any better.

And what did Mr. Christy O'Laighleis know about her or her world anyway? The very fact that he worked in the media probably meant that he only saw the "newsworthy" aspects of rock—the dumb, the dangerous. The calm, day-to-day hard work never made the news; the professionals who put in long, dedicated hours, who paid their bills and were looked on kindly by their neighbors, *they* never made the news. So, okay, she had been to a few—more than a few—parties where the fun had gotten out of hand. And she would admit that good people had gone down the drain before her very eyes, but to condemn a whole world for the excesses or weaknesses of a few was uncalled for.

So wrapped up in her internal argument was Robbie, it took her several songs to notice that Mairead was in total disarray. She hadn't warmed up properly, she missed her cues, she neglected to retune her guitar to each new key. The boys had stopped and started patiently several times, Robbie realized, and confined their annoyance to a few jokes and dark looks. They were a

nice bunch. But Mairead's head was definitely elsewhere. Robbie set herself to watch carefully and see if
she could identify the problem.

The song started again, a straightforward ballad with
a short bass solo. Mairead made it through two verses,
then drifted off during the bridge and failed to come
back in....

Micky threw down his drumsticks with a clatter while
Sean stared poker-faced at the floor. Eamonn finally
broke and cried, "Will you get your head out of the
trees, Mairead?"

"Oh stuff it, McInnes!" she snapped, uncharacteristically peevish.

Robbie knew she'd better step in. "Is there something on your mind, Mairead?"

"On her *mind*, it's not." The redheaded boy deftly
ducked the guitar pick that sliced toward his head.
"She's just heartbroken that she's not at the Armed
Forces' concert, mooning in the front row over Johnny
Kemp."

"I'm warning you, Eamonn!"

"Wait a minute! Wait a minute!" Robbie sought to
distract them from the developing battle. "If there was
a concert you wanted to see tonight why did we schedule this rehearsal?"

Mairead scuffed her foot in irritation. Her expression showed her to be more dispirited than Eamonn's
scorn would give her credit for. "Fact is, the tickets have
been sold out practically since the box office opened.
People camped out overnight in line."

"Are they doing any more shows in Dublin?"

"No, just tonight at the Showgrounds. Then they're
away back to America."

"Hmm, I didn't know they were even stopping in Ireland," Robbie mused, wondering whom she might know in the Armed Forces' contingent. Wasn't there someone from Simon's clique who managed their tours? Stu? Steve? What was his name? Steve Canova. Robbie slid decisively off the radiator where she had placed a cushion and briskly barked an order to her band, "Okay, rehearsal's over. Pack up."

"Huh?"

"How far away is this Showgrounds place?"

"Just a little ways beyond my brother's house in fact, but . . ."

"So we can be there in fifteen minutes by taxi, right? It's nearly nine-thirty, but we'll catch the last half of the show."

"But we don't have tickets!" Mairead reminded her, eyes gleaming with a reluctant hope.

"That just means we won't have seats. I hope you don't mind watching from the wings."

"How . . . you mean, you can get us in?"

"No promises, but the road manager may remember me."

The road manager did indeed remember her and took time to get them settled on folding chairs in front of the stage. Mairead was beside herself with excitement. Though she acted very nonchalant her hand shook when it touched Robbie's arm. "I'm naming my first-born daughter after you, Robbie!"

Robbie waved off her gratitude and shouted above the din. "It's nothing. What I can't figure out is why you never called Michael Shaw to see if *he* could pull some strings for you."

Her eyes grew very wide. "Why, it never occurred to me!"

Robbie blinked—such innocence! Maybe Christy was right to worry.

After the concert Robbie took her charges backstage to fraternize with the band, and went herself to thank Steve. They gossiped about industry rumors for a few minutes, then she let him escape to check on the gate receipts and she went back to her own band.

The boys were easy to find. They sat around companionably swilling beer with Armed Forces—at least *most* of Armed Forces. The lead singer, Johnny, was missing. So was Mairead. Robbie snooped around casually, looking for traces of a small blonde in a yellow sweatshirt, and found none.

Steve popped by to issue an invitation, including transportation, to the tour's wrap-up party at their hotel. Seeing Robbie's reluctance, one of the roadies pulled her aside and whispered confidentially, "If your girl is with Johnny they'll turn up at the hotel sooner or later. Johnny never misses a party." And so she let what was left of Fire Hazard pile into limousines and head for the hotel.

It was just the sort of party Robbie abhorred—too much liquor, too many illegal substances of all kinds, too many people acting like idiots. She noticed thankfully that her own band behaved themselves—all but Mairead who still hadn't shown up. She chewed her nails and kept her eyes open.

By three A.M. the boys had wisely crept off to their own homes, content to leave Robbie to recover their missing singer. At four-thirty the girl staggered in, giggling desperately and holding up a nearly comatose Johnny. Robbie bit off the opening words of the lecture she wanted to give. Mairead was in no condition to

absorb sense. She bundled the girl into the limo Steve
had kindly provided, and prayed during the whole way
to Christy's house for two things—that Mairead's giddy
drunk would not turn to a sick drunk in the car, and
that Christy was a very heavy sleeper. Had Mairead
been in better shape, she would have chanced taking her
to Howth rather than face her brother's accusations.
But it was touch and go even over the short stretch with
Mairead alternating between laughter and turning
green.

To Robbie's horror, when she succeeded in dragging
her charge into the Northumberland Road house, Mairead opened her mouth and bellowed at the top of her
well-developed lungs, "Oh, Christy! Brother darling!
I'm home!"

Robbie's head sank between her shoulders, unconsciously waiting for a blow to fall. Mairead yodeled
again, then harrumphed in disgust. "Hah, not home
yet, is he? The rogue..." She swayed toward the de-
scending staircase.

"Where are you going?"

"Breakfast," she answered airily. "'M hungry."

Robbie doubted that and skittered along in her wake
to save her from eating anything she'd regret.

They were still negotiating in the kitchen between hot
milk and beans on toast, the latter of which turned even
Robbie's sober stomach, when they heard the front
door open. Mairead put her finger to her lips and whispered in an exaggerated American accent, "Cheeze it—
the cops!" Then she stifled a fit of manic laughter.

Nothing about the situation struck Robbie as especially funny. She felt as if she had been caught in a
crime—contributing to the delinquency of a sister. True,
she could not have known, after one day's acquain-

tance, that Mairead had the common sense of a lemming, but Christy *had* warned her. *He* had known.

She waited dumbly for his entrance. His deep voice called questioningly down the stairwell and Robbie was struck by the warmth it held. "Mairead? Are you there, darling?" Then he appeared in the flesh and Robbie quelled an urge to slither under the table. His suit looked barely less crisp than it had remote hours ago, though the top buttons of his shirt had been undone and she fancied she could see the tracks of feminine fingers through his tousled hair. As soon as he took in the situation his jaw set in a grim line and his eyes narrowed to dashes of black.

Robbie brashly wiggled a few fingers at him in greeting. Mairead knocked over her warm milk. The ensuing scramble to mop it up gave Christy all the evidence he needed to know just how out of kilter his baby sister was. He observed them coldly as he strolled forward and sat on the table. Robbie found the edge of worry half-dulled by wonder at his beauty. The thigh nearest her, covered in taut cotton twill, was as muscled as that of an athlete, his waist lean and hard. He was all solid, lithe muscle, relaxed now and awaiting word from the dark brain behind his sable eyes.

"Had a bit of a time at rehearsal, did you?" he inquired carefully, laying a significant glance upon Robbie.

Tempted to lie, she kept silent. Mairead put on a grouchy, petulant face. "No, we didn't either. We went to a concert and a party afterward—friends of Robbie's."

Robbie could not imagine an explanation more calculated to damn her. She hated sitting there under the third degree of Christy's gaze like a criminal awaiting sentence, so she bared her teeth at him in a chilly half smile to see how he'd react. He didn't.

"Well." He pronounced the word like the toll of a bell. "Sounds like a busy day. You must be past ready for bed."

As if he had been her father, Mairead took that as an order. "In fact, I was just going up...." To Robbie's dismay she hustled herself toward the stairs, stopping by her brother long enough to receive his kiss on the top of her head, and then left Robbie alone with him.

She found that her body had started to sink into a craven sort of a crouch, like a dog waiting for its master to hit it. Ashamed of that reaction, she deliberately pulled herself up tall. Christy, in all truth, had made no move to touch her or even speak, he merely slid his sharp eyes from Mairead's retreating form to Robbie's. Their touch was keen edged as broken glass. It pricked her into an aggressive defense. "So," she began in her driest voice, climbing off the bench with exaggerated ease. "You didn't have long to wait for your proof—I'm even worse than you expected, aren't I? Your poor little sister, thrown to the wolves!" She made a show of rinsing out the cups in the white enamel sink. He watched, his cryptic silence doing great violence to her nerves.

"And you know, it gets worse. Oh, maybe you don't know—not being in rock. Oh yeah, as soon as Lawless Records gets the idea that she's The Next Big Thing, they're going to be trotting her off to parties like you wouldn't believe. And people are going to be trying to get on her good side, giving her things, being seen in her company, showing her a good time. Believe me, this is only the tip of the old rock and roll iceberg. Hanging about with scum like Simon Beyer, I've learned every depraved possibility.''

She checked to see if any of this melodramatic monologue had gotten through to him. She couldn't tell. He still sat there in sphinxlike mystery, hot as the golden desert, and as cool as the desert night. A little shiver ran through her. This was not the sort of sparring she wanted to do with him, not this angry, self-defensive stuff. She had thought often and longingly of their very first encounter, when each set of eyes, each wit, had tested the other and liked what it found. The memory made her doubly miserable.

She hooked her fingers into the waistband and belt loops of her jeans in order to hide the fact that they wanted to ball into fists, and strode up to him bravely. "It's everything you feared—drunks, drug addicts, sex fiends...." She leaned recklessly close, striving to put a little extra venom into her speech, since he had still not reacted. "And there I'll be, goading her into every step, immoral pervert that I am."

"Will you now?" he murmured thoughtfully. *Then* he reacted. His hard, brown arm went around her waist and toppled her onto his chest. He didn't even secure her with the other arm, one was enough—that and the implacable thighs pressed against each of her hips. The heat from his vital, radiant body, his hot, candle eyes drove a flush from her toes to her scalp. Her struggles to extricate her fingers from her own belt loops only worked her deeper into his embrace.

She yanked one hand free to slap ineffectually at his collarbone, the highest point she could reach, and he countered by anchoring his own hand in the hair at the nape of her neck and dragging her head back. She understood instantly that she had been set up for trouble, but as she took a gasping breath to protest, his mouth swallowed her words. His lips and teeth were potent warnings of his strength, as were the solid bands his arms made across her back. He gently bit her lips, preventing her from clenching her jaw shut, and then his tongue seared the inside of her mouth with his irresistible heat.

Simon had kissed her deeply, aggressively, but it had only made her mad. Christy's kiss made her mad and something else as well.... Confused? Regretful? Hungry? If he had kissed her like this two nights ago when his arm had nearly brushed her breast... If he had, then she would not now be locked rigid in his hostile arms, forcing herself not to flow into him like a spineless fool.

Through her lashes she could see his eyes, still shrewd and calculating, not a bit tormented by the passion that should inspire such a kiss. Even more appalled at herself, she made an aggrieved sound in her throat and dug her fingers into the hard muscle of his stomach.

He released her head and wrapped her hand in his own steely fingers. Free of his bruising mouth, she still could not back off without snapping her spine in half, but she had enough distance to glare at him poisonously.

"Very funny," she rasped in a strangled voice.

He replied coolly, "Very informative." At the question in her heated face, he raised one corner of his curved lips and said, almost apologetically, "Well, lass, I had to check."

Robbie felt all the blood leave her veins. He made an unnecessarily long production out of giving his judgment, easing the words out into the open, grinning ever more freely at their effect. "And perhaps...I was, um, unduly worried. Perhaps you're not as corrupt as I feared."

Furious, Robbie wrenched her other hand free and hit him. He grabbed her before she could swing a second time and held her firmly by the wrists. She stopped writhing.

"Now what was that for?" he demanded softly. "Because I misjudged you and you really *are* rotten to the core? Or because I've hurt your pride?"

Suddenly the humor of the situation struck her. "I don't know. You've given me a lot of choices, haven't you? Any of them will do."

His face brightened as if a light had been switched on behind his eyes. He was too handsome to look at directly, too overwhelming to be ignored. She heard his voice rumble into her hair, much softer and more coaxing than ever before. "I certainly didn't mean to suggest that you couldn't *learn* to be corrupt. I *did* tell you I was a fairly good teacher."

And this time, slowly, using only the power of his warmth and magnetic appeal, he drew her forward into a gentle kiss. It was nothing like its rough predecessor. The only savagery was the wild emotion that tore through her as his lips drifted over hers, caressing the curves, hypnotizing her with sweet sensations. She sighed and tugged free her hands to hold his dark-gold head between her palms. When his own hand pulled her closer into his chest she softened like clay. When his tongue played over the edges of her teeth she parted them, welcoming his intoxicating taste.

One ever protective part of her remained alert for any coercive move, but he held himself to the most careful, exploratory of kisses, testing at every step what scared her and what seduced her. Then, long before she was ready, he let her go.

For a fraction of a second her dazed mind thought she saw something equally dazed in his eyes. Could he have been the tiniest bit surprised by some reaction of his own, some treacherous softness for her, perhaps? But when she found the wits to look again, after hauling herself rigorously out of his arms, she saw only his familiar, slightly amused scrutiny. *She* felt as if a big log had fallen out of the sky onto her head, yet *he* sat unmoved and observed her as an engineer would the dials of a fascinating new machine.

She would have been unprepared for any of the things he could have said next. The one he did say floored her.

"Shall I call you a taxi?"

As casual as that! Two shattering kisses and then "Shall I call you a taxi?" Robbie gasped from inarticulate anger and stiffened her arms at her sides—hitting him had already proved useless. She felt frazzled and shrill. "Is this your equivalent of sending me off to bed like Mairead? Because if it is, rest assured that no matter *how* you treat me, I am *not* your little sister!"

"I know," he agreed in a perfectly rational voice. "The thought that came to me, actually, was not to send you off to *bed*, but to *my* bed." At her sudden lack of retorts he had the effrontery to cock an ironic eyebrow and continue. "Then I realized I'd be doing myself and Mairead no favor by teaching you what's behind all the talk you spout. The less you know, the less you can teach her. So, darlin', it's best you go home."

Robbie could think of no argument that would gain her footing in this impossible bog. She snatched her jacket and bag from the chair beside him, careful not to pass too close lest her rage set his clothes on fire. She stormed upstairs. His solicitous, mocking offer followed after her. "Shall I call you that taxi then?"

Outside the cracklingly crisp dawn air was in bright contrast to her mood. Robbie had always regarded her even temper as one of her greatest assets. Christy O'Laighleis has knocked down *that* vanity. Somewhere in her flustered gray matter she *must* have a bit of rationality left, a shred of the civilized person she had once been. How had Christy managed to do this to her? She could not simply bury the incident in some disregarded corner of her consciousness, she had to figure it out.

The only other man who had ever provoked her so had been Simon.... The whole mess became embarrassingly clear.

When Simon Beyer had first swept into Soho Sound Studios, as sharply dressed and cool-eyed as any photo in a British rock magazine, the seventeen-year-old Robbie had discovered the first interest of her life that rivaled music. He was sleek and charming, petted by everyone from record company executives to an even more awesome eminence—the head engineer. Simon brought big names to work at Soho, energized the place with his adrenalin-charged, partying, jet-set life-style. Robbie had suffered a severe, bewildering crush.

Seeing him always surrounded by stylish women, she never expected him to notice her. So she was not overly surprised when the notice he did take of her was as innocent and platonic as that of a big brother for a little sister. It pleased him to take her on as his protégée. He skipped her right out of the engineering career she had plotted out for herself and made her his assistant.

She had taken to producing as a bird takes to the sky. At first she spent all her time photocopying contracts for the unionized session musicians and preparing song lists for the mastering labs. She never complained, indeed she was in heaven. When she later found herself patching up Simon's relationships with the more fractious stars, and covering for him at sessions when he showed up late and bleary-eyed, she took it in her stride. She even accepted a few little projects on the side—demos mostly, for unknown performers. It was exhilarating.

After two and one half years of close but placid work together, she noticed that Simon's behavior toward her was changing. From a fond, if moody, teacher he metamorphosed into a suitor. Their time alone together passed less in discussions about noise reduction and more in silly chatter and sweet kisses. The old crush flared up.

Robbie tried valiantly to enjoy it with no doubts or worries as to why Simon had suddenly discovered this passion. But two things kept her from falling into his arms as carelessly as she wished she could—the first *was* indeed that suspicion about his change of heart; the second was guilt over her own growing success. She had established a reputation of her own, more and more people were willing to risk her inexperience for the talent she showed—and of course the inexperience was naturally decreasing. More and more offers came in; more and more they interfered with her work for Simon.

Then she finally saw through the haze of love and realized that her mentor's career was slipping. A producer in pop music usually had a short flare of prominence, like the stars he produced. Most had their brief time at the top of the charts and then slipped into the less glamorous, steadier fields of music. Many left to become record company executives themselves or promoters or deejays.

Simon wouldn't let go of the top. He refused to admit that he, too, might have to slide off the peak. For a long while he had kept Robbie from seeing the truth. He took such an interest in her projects that she was flattered, relieved that he was not resentful or jealous. Though his training would influence her for the rest of her life, she had developed her own ear. She liked an entirely different sort of music; her touch in the studio produced an entirely different aural signature.

When she finally let the veil fall from her eyes, the truth left her feeling hollow and betrayed. Simon knew long before she did herself that he might no longer be on the cutting edge of music, however determined he had been to avoid the knowledge, *but she was.* He had sensed her slipping away from him into a hot career of her own and had sought to keep his hand in. His romancing had boiled down to that—keeping his hand in.

Simon had been her first human passion. She intended for him to be her last. Life flowed smoothly when she could rely on her sane, civilized habits to keep the world in perspective and in control. When emotion clouded her judgment she was as stupid and helpless as any natural-born fool. No more of that!

It had been a nice plan, but imperfect—it had not taken into consideration one Christy O'Laighleis. Robbie didn't kid herself about what she had felt in his arms. It was passion—no question about that. It might not have been backed up by years of fond acquaintance and girlish sentiment, but it had certainly unplugged her common sense for a few unbelievable moments. Why else had she allowed him to kiss her a *second* time? A fever washed through her head at the memory. *He* was the dangerous one. He had gotten her so turned around that her brain, if it could have been played aloud, would have sounded like a tape run backward.

Thinking about him had led her astray in more than one way. Robbie looked around her and decided she was either on Flatbush Avenue in Brooklyn or she was lost. The pretty little streets of spick-and-span red brick had been replaced by gray warehouses and grimy shop-fronts. She could have been in any industrial American city.

Sighing, she dug the map out of her bag and pre-tended to scan it. Within moments two middle-aged la-dies appeared to direct her back to the Gresham. Their kindness was a balm to her soul after the rough morn-ing. Dublin might not be the fairy-tale city it had seemed at first, but it had its points.

Chapter Four

If Michael Shaw hadn't called the next day, Robbie would have slept on through lunch and forgotten the apartments Mairead had scheduled her to see.

"Oh, Michael! What time is it? Do I have time to get to a place called Sandymount Road by one o'clock?"

Briefly she explained her situation, wondering what could have happened to Mairead—they had planned to go together. Then again, with the size of the hangover Mairead was likely to have, perhaps her company would have to be sacrificed.

"You should have come to me for help in this, Robbie. That's what I'm here for." Michael sounded aggrieved.

"I was going to. These appointments just sort of came up on the spur of the moment."

"Look, I'll stop by the Gresham and fetch you. If these places won't do, I know of some others farther out of town."

"All right, thanks. I'll try and get hold of Mairead."

Robbie's trepidation over placing a call to Christy's house turned out to be wasted—no one answered. Likewise Howth. Evidently Mairead had recovered enough to be out and about, if not to have remembered Robbie's appointments.

She had to hustle to get ready: shower, throw on clothes and a dash of makeup, look into her bag to see that it held supplies for another day. But every time her mind slipped away from necessary thoughts it chose to fiddle with troubling ones. Now in the clear, cool noon of this northern city, Robbie found the events of the previous night, or rather that very morning, quite un-believable. If anything so dramatic and bizarre had ac-tually happened, surely she wouldn't be walking around now unchanged, cleaning out her hairbrush, putting the caps back on her pens. Alone with herself Robbie hardly knew how she felt. She was absurdly grateful at the prospect of Michael's company; she hoped it would distract her.

He picked her up in a roomy Mercedes sedan, the type of car bound to make an impression on the bands he courted for Lawless. A tidy, baby-faced man in his early thirties, he brought with him only a tinge of the New York circus where she had first met him. His En-glish-inflected brogue had seemed quaint then. Now in his native surroundings that accent and the American-isms in his speech struck Robbie as incongruous. She thought how bland he sounded compared to the pep-pery Mairead.

"How are you enjoying Dublin?" he inquired as he helped her into the car.

She used this as her cue to start a line of pleasant small talk that carried them through the rest of the afternoon.

With Michael as her guide she made her three appointments with no trouble or confusion. Unfortunately none of the places suited her. It was nearly as discouraging as looking for apartments in New York, except that the landlords invariably offered her tea.

The modern apartment blocks Michael suggested depressed her further and made her think longingly of the gracious houses.

"Have you a rehearsal scheduled with the band tonight?" Michael asked at the end of their travels.

"Yes—that is, if Mairead hasn't died from her drinking bout."

"Do you want to go back to the hotel for a nap or can I talk you into dinner?"

"My gosh, is it that late?"

"It's five. A bit early by New York standards but..."

"But none too soon for someone who hasn't eaten yet today. You don't have to talk me into anything, I'll drive the car!"

He took her to a tiny restaurant tucked into a side street. She felt underdressed in her shirt and jeans until the waiter's friendly welcome reassured her. Then she settled herself around a glass of crisp white wine and put the question of apartments out of her mind. She and Michael fell naturally into industry talk.

"Have you read any of the music trades recently?" he inquired, wearing a mysterious smile.

"No, I hardly ever bother. It'd just make me paranoid."

"It shouldn't—you've had at least two albums in the top one hundred for the past year."

"Yeah, but what goes up must come down."

Michael shook his head in wonder. "So modest. How are you getting along with Fire Hazard?"

"Oh, great. They're real sweet. And you're right, they've got a very modern edge to their sound and they're tight. I don't anticipate any problems in the studio...." Unless Mairead causes trouble, Robbie amended silently.

"Except?"

"Huh?"

"I thought I heard a little quaver of doubt in your voice. Are you having any kind of trouble at all?"

"Well, not with the band per se... but I'm wondering... maybe I'm overreacting..."

Michael waited for her to go on.

"Mairead's got this disapproving older brother who really thinks rock is the lowest form of depravity known to man, and I think that Mairead acts up a little *because* he's so negative. I wish someone could tell him to ease up on her. I wish I understood why he has such a grudge."

"Ah, the infamous Christy O'Laighleis."

The sound of the last name, pronounced in her presence for the first time, drew Robbie's head up. "Yes, do you know him?"

"Oh, there's hardly anybody in the business in Ireland who doesn't know him." Michael rolled his eyes.

Robbie's imagination scrambled to understand how Christy could have made himself so notorious as a government consultant.

Michael continued. "When I found out whose sister she was I could hardly believe she had a band. I would have expected Chris to lock her up in a convent or something."

"Isn't that a bit extreme? I mean, I've heard of being protective but . . ."

"Oh, yeah, I have to remind myself that he's not such a monster. After all, he *could* have destroyed Lawless a few years ago and he chose not to. But old impressions die hard, I suppose, and I got used to thinking of him as a *very* formidable boss."

Robbie put her hand on his arm to capture his attention away from the veal on his plate. "Wait a minute, Michael. I get the feeling I'm missing something here. When was he your boss?"

The bland A & R man blinked. "Back when Lawless was still his company."

"His company?" Robbie's brain struggled. O'Laighleis . . . Lawless . . . They did sound very similar. One must be the Irish of the other.

"Oh, I'm sorry, Robbie. It's absurd of me to expect that all our internecine warfare is known to the rest of the world. You see, he's only gone by Christy O'Laighleis since he gave up trying to reconstruct the entire Irish rock establishment. Before that he was Chris Lawless, Irish great white hope. He started Lawless Records in the early seventies—I think he was all of twenty-one— so that the really progressive new native bands wouldn't have to sign with foreign companies. This was even before the big explosion of independent labels in Britain. He was ahead of himself in more ways than one."

Robbie was stunned. Her omelet sat before her untouched. "I can't believe it! He *founded* Lawless?"

"And ran it, too—like a dictator. He oversaw every wrinkle of work from the signing of new acts to the gluing together of the record jackets at the pressing plant. He did so much work that some of us—I was in promotion then—began to suspect that he had himself cloned.''

Robbie choked, thinking of stereo Christys.

"Even later when we expanded and he had to delegate responsibility, he still managed to know what was going on in every corner and to turn up in your office just when you were least prepared to see him. It was uncanny.''

"Well, what happened?''

"Just what any entrepreneur hopes for, unless he's Chris Lawless. The company got successful. He started expanding into related areas—distribution, actual recording, pressing. He wanted to extend his own exacting standards to the entire industry, but of course that required more capital than even he could raise on his own and he ended up selling part interest in the company to several big corporations. He figured he could essentially stay in control because he still had the biggest chunk of stock.''

"I take it this didn't happen.''

"No. Well, it hardly could—Lawless was too damn profitable. One of the corporations bought out the others and started putting some very heavy pressure on Chris. They wanted him to merge with a British company they owned, and they tried to get in on artistic decisions. He battled out every single move they made, but it was not what you'd call a rewarding way of life for him anymore—all corporate cloak and dagger, no time to spend on the music. Finally he sold his stock for a bundle and told them to go hang themselves with it.''

"From the looks of the company, I'd say they didn't take his advice about that, either.''

Michael looked thoughtful, a bit bemused. "Well...I guess you could say that. But from another angle they sort of *did*. I mean, look at what we're doing now—our whole artistic and sales philosophy is to go after the big established markets, so we've had to dig around through Ireland for what are essentially American and British bands. We've gotten so dependent on the outside network we can't let our acts give an interview to the Cork *Examiner* without consulting the London office.''

"And I'm a part of that...." she murmured gloomily.

Michael leaped to rescue her spirits. "Nonsense! It has nothing to do with you—it's a corporate policy. The music is still valid, even if it isn't 'Irish' by Christy's standards. It doesn't matter who makes what music where. No corporate policy is going to turn Fire Hazard into something they aren't. And actually, sister or not, Mairead would never have gotten a recording contract with Lawless when Chris ran it. So, who's to judge?''

"Still...you're evidently committed to Lawless's current policy, and yet you sounded sort of sad just now explaining the downfall of its old policy.''

He smiled ruefully, then shrugged. "Oh, just the sentimental Irishman in me, I guess. I've no great need to single-handedly recreate Irish culture like Christy has, but still and all—he made a proper go of it. For a few years there Lawless was something very special.''

"And you said he could have destroyed it rather than just letting go?''

"Yes, he could have ripped it to shreds from the inside. Even at the end he had that much power. But he just walked away. He's actually *not* vindictive or vengeful, just very firm in his own convictions.''

"'Firm...''' she repeated wryly. "Yeah, I guess I'd go along with that.''

Robbie couldn't believe her luck when Michael turned the Mercedes down Crown Alley. It looked as if her newly acquired understanding of Christy O'Laighleis would be put to the test shortly. His little red car sat at the curb.

"Uh-oh."

"Did you say something?" Michael asked.

"Speak of the devil. That's Christy's car."

Michael reached over to pat her shoulder comfortingly. "Don't worry, I'll protect you."

His gallant offer sounded lightweight in the face of Christy's hostility. Michael didn't take their conflict as seriously as Robbie did. Of course he wouldn't—she hadn't told him *everything*.

She gathered her composure with every intention of sauntering upstairs, protected by the new sympathy Michael's insights had inspired in her, when her treacherous limbs froze. Christy strode out from beneath the archway heading for his car. He gave the Mercedes a quick glance, then he stopped and looked again. The dark slashes of his eyes narrowed further. Robbie struggled with the conflicting feelings that bashed through her like contrary storms. She had never met anyone so intimidating, one disdainful curl of his expressive mouth made her want to slither into the toes of her boots. Yet another part of her fixed on every glimpse of him with vital attention.

Before Michael could notice her rigidity, Robbie managed to coax some movement from her limbs. She forced herself onto the sidewalk. Without the car's heavy door between her and the man who believed her to be his antagonist, she felt eerily vulnerable. As if he knew to the last degree just *how* vulnerable, Christy intensified his hot stare.

Understanding, she reminded herself. You know exactly why he thinks you're dangerous now—it's not random, it's not personal. It's based on a very noble idea he has for the land he loves. This silent lecture helped.

"Well, hello, Christy!" Michael sang out gaily. "Have you come to hear one of your sister's rehearsals tonight?"

Robbie cringed. Have Christy glowering at the back of her neck all evening while she tried to run a rehearsal? She didn't think her resistance would hold up.

Christy's answer came like a break in a heat wave. "I've just dropped her off. She hardly needs a pesty brother making her nervous, don't you think, Michael? Or are you so anxious to lose your—Lawless investment?"

Robbie couldn't tell if his mention of Lawless carried an emphasis that meant something special to Michael or if she was just touchy. The subtle shifts in Lawless politics, until this very evening a total mystery to her, still evaded her grasp, so she followed Michael's lead and ignored all innuendo. Instead, she grinned as if she and Christy had never shared the slightest strain between them. "I think Mairead is up to your scrutiny. She's a tough cookie."

In a wondering tone of voice, Christy repeated, "'A tough cookie?'" and Robbie realized it must not be a standard Irish phrase.

She plowed ahead "Anyway, you're more than welcome to sit in on a session." Then she tried something that felt a tiny bit foolhardy. "Michael's been filling me in on your background. I hadn't realized that Mairead's interest in music was a family trait." She might have said "rock" rather than just "music," but that would have *really* needled him.

Her remark, however diluted, made him draw himself up tighter. "Then perhaps my concerns no longer seemed quite so unreasonable to you."

"Theoretically," she conceded.

Dissatisfied with her answer Christy snapped open the door of his car and got in. "I'll not hold you up any longer. Good night."

Michael and Robbie exchanged perplexed looks, then the A & R man reached out to his own door handle. "Cheerio, Robbie. I'll keep working on finding you a flat. If you need anything else—transportation, moral support—just give me a call. You have my home phone number don't you?"

"Yes. Thanks, Michael. Good night." She waved after the departing Mercedes.

Christy still had not gone. He rustled unproductively through the papers on the seat next to him. Feeling a sudden rush of audacity, Robbie walked to the curb beside him and squatted down, her two hands on the top of the door. Astonished, Christy looked up and, for the space of one heartbeat, Robbie thought she saw a hint of yearning in his sable eyes. Yearning for what? Whatever it was, it gave her the guts to go on.

"Come up to the rehearsal tonight, Christy. You *know* your opinion means a lot to Mairead." Her nerve started to fail her at that point; the last part of her plea was fractured by hesitation. "Maybe she thinks you disapprove of her. Maybe that's why she gets a little ... rebellious once in a while. Maybe if ..."

"*Maybe* you should review the terms of your contract with Lawless Records, Ms. Calderón," he warned quietly. "Does it really include family counseling?"

Blanching, she pulled her hands back from the car. If there had been any chance of reaching a conciliatory truce with Christy, she had blown it. She watched as he roughly put the car in gear and accelerated away.

Everybody had managed to make it to the rehearsal that evening, even Mairead, who still looked a little green and more than a little sheepish. Robbie beamed at them all, refusing to let the encounter with Christy affect her relationship with the band. It would have been so easy to become a drill sergeant; she felt ten years older and wiser than they were...well, maybe not *wiser*. But she refused to fall into the role, even though it might have been the exact way to endear herself to Christy. Too late for that, she sighed, their relationship had taken too weird a turn—a turn into a blind alley, as far as she could tell.

Things were so much more complicated than they seemed at first, she thought in amazement. Christy must find unpleasant irony in the fact that his own sister had fallen to the lure of the world he rejected, that she was denying her unique Irish birthright even as he fought to protect it. No wonder he was bitter.

But *was* he bitter or just all too aware of the realities of that life? He obviously knew it in intimate detail, and lately Robbie had come to see that Mairead was a bit too giddy to inspire total confidence.

The girl wasn't giddy tonight. She put her hand to her cropped head once or twice as if to still a pounding headache, but went on with the songs valiantly. She hit every note, remembered every word and every cue, even though she lacked her usual pizzazz. Robbie let her suffer. If she had never faced the repercussions of a drinking bout, it was past time she did so. Meanwhile, the rest of the band was in fine form.

By the time they took a break Robbie felt they had made up for the aborted rehearsal the previous day. The boys had brought food and Guinness, so they stayed in for supper. Everyone lounged about the comfortably seedy loft, chatting about musician friends and the instruments they would buy when they were rich. Mairead surreptitiously took two aspirins and put a damp cloth over her face. The boys rolled their eyes at one another.

To distract them before they said anything of a teasing nature, Robbie started talking about Donal and Emerald. They pricked up their ears right away; even Mairead discarded the cloth.

"You know, I've only heard a few hours of your rehearsals, but you're tight and the arrangements are solid. If you feel ready I'm sure I could get you into the studio a week or two early. Donal said they're booked very lightly right now. How about it?"

After a few timid comments and much exchanging of eager looks they agreed that they did feel ready to record. They had been playing the same songs for months, perfecting them; the rehearsals were more for Robbie's benefit. But she had a very quick ear and a keen memory for music. A couple more nights and she'd know every song note for note.

"Okay, great. I'll talk to Donal about starting sooner. I think you should have a tour of the place, too, so everything is less unfamiliar when you actually get in there to work."

Micky, ever organized, said, "We've got the next couple of days free since we weren't going to rehearse over the weekend."

"Then let's plan on tomorrow afternoon. I'll call Donal and ask him to open the place up for us—tomorrow is Saturday, isn't it? Or have I lost track? Okay, tomorrow afternoon—twoish. What's the matter, Mairead?"

The singer stared guiltily at her toes. "Uh, well . . . since we hadn't a rehearsal scheduled I thought I'd . . . that is, Johnny, you know—in Armed Forces—asked me along on a wee trip. He and the other fellows were going up to Donegal for a bit of the sea. It was just until Tuesday—I'd have been back for the next rehearsal, but I'd miss the tour."

Robbie bit her tongue so she wouldn't say anything. Eamonn and Micky said it for her.

"What, are you joining Armed Forces then? Are we not your band anymore, Mairead?"

The singer bristled. "It's only a bit of fun, Hennessey! Just three bloody days!"

"Yeah, and *if* you drag yourself the whole rocky way from the West on Tuesday, will you show up again with a head like an eggshell?"

"It's none of your bloody business how I spend my free time, is it now?"

"It is if we're a band. How will it be on tour, us not knowing when you're going to skip off with some lad or other?"

Mairead snarled out an unrecognizable curse. "You're quite the hand of justice, aren't you? Worse than my own brother! Hanging me before I've even committed the crime."

"Ach, don't be so dramatic." Micky turned away disgustedly. "Just decide if you're going or you aren't."

"Thanks very much. You've made it very clear that my own decision isn't good enough for you. Will you listen to Robbie then? Shall we let *her* decide?"

Robbie's mouth dropped open in speechless protest. Micky snapped back, "Will *you*?"

"Aye," Mairead declared. "What do you think, Robbie?"

"I think you shouldn't use me to decide band business. When you're out on the road I won't be there, just the four of you. Remember that."

"But you must have an opinion—we'd respect that."

"Oh, I've got lots of opinions. And one of them is that we'd better run through those last two songs again to make sure we're all clear on the chord progressions. If we have to start from scratch at the next rehearsal because no one bothered to memorize the changes, I'll show you my mean and nasty side."

She refused either to be sucked into arbitrating their dispute or letting them fall back into it during rehearsal. Lots of bands had personal altercations, but if the music was given top priority much could be smoothed over. She dragged them relentlessly back to their places. The two songs proceeded roughly with a few spiky comments as mistakes were made, but when Robbie later called time she felt they had cooled off fairly well. They would not leap at each other's throats the minute she left them alone.

At the end of rehearsal Mairead followed her down the steps into the still, cool night. "Robbie, wait!"

Knowing what was coming, Robbie turned and braced herself.

"You won't be angry if I go off with Johnny, will you? It's only three days. I think *they're* just old crabs, or jealous or something."

"Honey, it's really not important whether I'm mad or not. I'm working for *you* guys, you know—Fire Hazard. Fire Hazard decides things, I just help the music out."

The girl looked sullen, and touchingly young. Robbie suddenly felt the weight of experience descend upon her. "All right, I understand what you're saying, Robbie. But it would help *me* to know your opinion. I mean, I've never been asked out by a rock star before. Maybe it's turned my head and I'm not thinking straight."

Robbie felt this was a rather mature admission for so young a girl. Perhaps Mairead would shape up after all. "Well, think of it this way—if Fire Hazard becomes a major band you'll get invited out by so many big shots you'll get bored. But if Fire Hazard is going to bomb, maybe you should take whatever chances you get to have fun."

Mairead frowned crossly. "We're not going to bomb! We're good! You said so yourself, that we had it!"

"So I did. Well, shouting it into a deserted street won't set your fate in concrete one way or the other. I'm going home to bed. Good night."

Christy looked up when the front door slammed; he heard footsteps but no small sister poked her head in the doorway to say hello. That wasn't like her.

"Mairead?" he called. "Is it you or a crazed murderer?"

For his answer he got an inaudible grumble. What could have happened to make his buoyant sister so surly? Concerned, he laid down the newspaper and wandered out into the hall. She stood by the telephone, skimming the notepad for messages. She looked up, her face tired and unhappy. "What? Christy O'Casanova home on a Saturday night? Do I feel the earth shudder from shock?"

He detected troubled feelings beneath the sarcasm and made sure to give a mild reply. "Ah well, it gets tiring sometimes—going out."

She slapped down the pad in disgust, "I wouldn't know. *I* don't have your exhausting social life."

Before she stormed off he asked gently, "Darling, what's the matter? Did your rehearsal not go well?"

"Aw, Christy, everyone's ganging up on me.... It's enough to make one paranoid."

"Who's everyone?"

"The band, Robbie, *everyone*.

She sounded so disgusted he tucked her against his side and walked her into the living room. "Seems to me you've held your own with the boys in the past. No Lawless ever let a bunch of skinny guitarists push him around."

She managed a wan smile. "Oh, I can handle them...it's Robbie."

Christy controlled his tremor of curiosity. Yesterday his little sibling had been positively in *love* with her cool, cosmopolitan American producer, quoting her at length, digging through his record collection to listen to singers the woman had recommended. He had done his best to downplay this enthusiasm. All Mairead needed was another bad role model—he himself had already caused enough damage in that department.

"But now? Disgruntled?"

Mairead sighed fatalistically. "All I wanted to do was go off on a bit of a jaunt—it wouldn't even have interfered with the rehearsal schedule. And all of a sudden everyone looks like I've murdered their best friend.

Robbie was the worst, she sounds like you're giving her lessons."

As little as he liked to think of someone browbeating a member of his family, a flash of something like approval ignited at Mairead's words. "So your darling producer sided with the rest of the band against you?"

"Worse—she gave me the old 'personal responsibility' routine."

Christy sputtered, not quite able to quell his burst of laughter. Mairead glared at him and he quickly plastered a sympathetic expression onto his face. "Appealed to your conscience, did she? May God forgive her."

Mairead's accusing look slowly transformed itself into one of humor. "Pretty mean, huh?"

He nodded, "Abominable."

"Yeah, I thought so." She sprang up from the couch, a much more cheerful being than the one who had slouched into the room. "I'm pooped—I'm going to bed." She added, a note of self-mockery in her tone, "It's tiring being so mature."

He gazed after her in affection. Yes, it certainly was tiring; he himself had only recently realized how tiring it was trying to be "God's voice on earth," as a certain American had put it.

So, the American had a reasonable bone or two in her young and distressingly appealing body.... A wave of guilt swept him. Perhaps he had been less than fair. Could he be jealous? He couldn't change the fact that a new influence had walked into Mairead's life, but he had a responsibility to determine just what sort of influence the woman would prove to be. So far he had judged her on the tiniest scrap of evidence and a lot of prejudice. He didn't like to think of himself as a bigot but . . .

Perhaps he should have gone to the rehearsal as she had suggested. Perhaps he should make a point of going to one in the near future. It might not serve the purpose Robbie's amateur psychology suggested it would, but he'd have a chance to observe her effect on his sister.

He groaned dismally. He was starting to fall for the kind of phony logic he detected in politicians every day. It made perfect sense to go to a rehearsal telling himself he did it for himself. He simply, inexplicably, wanted to see more of Robbie Calderón.

The next day Fire Hazard met Robbie at Emerald—all of them. No one made any temperamental remarks so she guessed that they had settled the Donegal affair amicably. She was pleased.

Though it was Donal's day off, he stuck around and chatted the band through a tour. They responded well to his friendly manner. Luck had sent Robbie a good combination of personalities to work with.

Michael Shaw, who must have absorbed some of Christy's ESP from the old Lawless days to know where they were, showed up later to give the band a dose of corporate encouragement. His business-suited presence reminded them that their music was no longer just a hobby for friends to believe in and parents to tolerate. It had the very tangible backing of an aggressive prestigious company, even if it wasn't the company Christy had at first envisioned. . . .

Why should that bother her? She and Christy were hardly deathless friends, guarding each other's dreams as their own. In many ways, they were working against each other. She wouldn't go so far as to say they were *enemies*. No, never enemies. She would never let things between them deteriorate to that point. After all, he was still Mairead's brother.

On Monday Robbie used her freedom to roam around Dublin, ostensibly looking for apartments. She spent more time wondering about Christy, especially while she ate ice cream in an oddly melancholy little park called the Garden of Remembrance. It commemorated those who had fallen fighting for Irish independence. Was that what Christy was doing—fighting for the independence of Irish hearts and minds in their music?

She decided that sitting surrounded by the engraved names of dead freedom fighters was making her maudlin. She licked the last drips of ice cream off her fingers and set out for her hotel. Another night in a hotel would cure her of such romantic nonsense.

What cured her even more quickly was the sight of a tall, golden blond nodding to the Gresham's doorman as he headed for a red sports car. What was Christy doing at her hotel? He spied her before she could decide if she wanted to face him or run. Hands in the pockets of his spotless, apricot-colored linen suit, he waited at the curb.

"Well, hi," she said coolly, sure that he could see the knot her stomach had just become.

"You've a good day for walking." His dark eyes swept the sunny street scene. "You must have brought the dry weather with you from New York. We're usually half-hidden in mist and rain—like Brigadoon."

Probably the only good he'd say she had brought with her, Robbie commented to herself. But what was this talk of weather? Could the autocratic, disapproving (the word "dictatorial" came to mind) Mr. O'Laighleis be nervous? In *her* presence? It was probably some ploy to throw her off balance, but the temptation to believe that he was the one who felt off balance proved irresistible. She slouched to a halt before him. "It doesn't seem to have affected your tan."

"What?" She thought she saw a rosy flush start up under that very tan. He put an impulsive hand up to his face. "Oh, well, I spend the odd weekend in the sun— Portugal."

"Ah." She was enjoying the momentary rest from his hard eyes. "So, is there some problem? Is Mairead all right?"

"Oh, fine, fine. No, there's no problem at all." He shifted uncomfortably from one stylish Italian leather shoe to the other. "Mairead mentioned that you were eager to move into a flat. Have you found one?"

"No. Looks like I'm stuck here with the Aga Khan."

A tentative smile flashed into his marvelous eyes. Then seriousness settled upon him again. "I've learned of something that might do you. The landlady is a lovely woman— I've already told her about you."

"And she's still willing to rent to me?"

This time he paled. He stared at his toes for a moment before bringing his eyes up to meet hers. "I've been a bit rough on you, I know. I've had no right.... If I could make it up in some way..."

"Okay, how about a couple hundred thousand pounds, the keys to your car and your firstborn male child?"

For a second he looked stunned. Then he grinned and tossed a rattling object into her hands—his keys! "I've me checkbook with me," he explained. "The last will have to wait a while."

Chapter Five

The apartment was perfect. It occupied the top floor in one of the double houses along Northumberland and offered a bedroom, sitting room, tiny kitchen and bath with a lion-footed tub. The furniture was old, well cared for and comfortable enough that Robbie didn't feel she had to perch delicately on the edges of the chairs.

Mrs. Hall, the spindly, eighty-year-old landlady, clucked over Robbie's misfortune of having to live in a hotel and chided her for not having brought her suitcase with her. Robbie felt so at home she, too, wished she could skip the trip back to the Gresham. She wanted to curl up on the settee holding a cup of strong, sweet tea and spend the rest of the afternoon looking out over Mrs. Hall's flower garden.

The settling of the lease seemed to be no more than the old lady patting her on the arm. "That's grand, dear. I'm glad to have any friend of Christy's in this house. I'll be giving you the key now."

Any friend of Christy's...Robbie smiled blandly and said nothing. Christy had been kind and cheery from the moment she set off with him from the Gresham. It would have been very easy to slip into a careless frame of mind, one in which she might be tempted to think they were friends. He certainly acted that way, treating her to a funny commentary on the sights and smells of Dublin as they drove, pointing out the bus stops and dealers within walking distance of Mrs. Hall's, taking her arm as she alighted from car to curb.

She was afraid to look the truth straight in the face, she knew it would pounce on her soon enough when she left his company—they were *not* friends, their relationship was in limbo. He might no longer abhor her—for some mysterious reason—but he was a long way from seeking her out by choice. Mairead still provided their only real link.

Mairead and the fact that they now lived on the same block.

"There's a grocer's a few short blocks from here," Christy commented while they headed for the red sports car. "While you have the buggy and driver would you like to lay in a few supplies? Would you prefer to check out of the Gresham and then shop?"

She sobered. She could detect nothing in his face but an earnest desire to cart her through the domestic chores of her life, but she knew that was too good to be true. He probably had seven dates lined up for that evening.

"Oh, thank you, but I won't hold you up anymore." She cut him off as he opened his mouth to protest, "It was above and beyond the call of duty rescuing me from hoteldom. Some people get large fees for this."

His smile warmed her like a glow of sunshine. "I'll be well paid if you just keep taking good care of my sister."

"Keep taking good care?" Afraid she'd end up sounding sarcastic, she said no more.

"I could have talked to her until I talked a hole into the wall, and she would have shied off to Donegal with that light lad of hers, but she didn't go."

"Well, that's *it*—your talking to her."

"What do you mean?"

"You've already done all your youthful experimenting and she feels like you're denying her the opportunity to do hers."

He nodded, making strands of golden hair fall over a face that was dark with self-reproach. "Aye, the best of intentions . . ." he murmured. "Funny how they do go astray."

Robbie said nothing, knowing that his astray intentions included not only his hopes for Mairead but those long ago for Lawless Records. He wasn't the type to quit and fall into bitter despair; he was the type to back up, lick his wounds and, with those sly, canny eyes of his, spy out a new angle.

"She *is* a good kid," Robbie reminded him.

"She is at that. I've never had a moment's doubt."

"And I really had nothing to do with her decision not to go to Donegal. I just suggested she keep in mind her responsibilities to the band—*she* had to come to the decision."

"Then you've a finer touch than I, Ms. Calderón. I should be encouraging you to stick by her rather than scaring you off with my barbaric manners."

Robbie laughed in genuine mirth. "It would take more than a little disapproval to pry me out of Ireland right now. And please call me Robbie."

He pulled up to the familiar blue awnings of the Gresham, her doorstep for the last time. "Robbie, then. Ah, here we are, your former home."

The sound of her name from his throat, the soft, rolling *r*, the breathy rumble of the rest, seemed to reveal, for the first time, the way her name was meant to be pronounced. By the time he appeared on her side to open the door she had recovered from the effect. "Thank you, Christy—for everything." She was afraid to imbue the word with all the significance she meant.

He seemed to take it harmlessly. "You're certainly welcome. I've no qualms about leaving you in Mrs. Hall's hands."

"Or her in mine?"

"Or that."

"Thanks. Well, good night." Then she perversely took a risk. "I hope I haven't made you keep Aideen waiting. Or is it Helena?"

He answered without missing a beat, "Peggy."

Christy had gotten her into a flat just in time, Robbie knew. As soon as Fire Hazard started recording she had no time to comb the city for digs and no emotional resilience to cóntinue on at the hotel. She ran the sessions as if they were training for the Olympics, pushing the band hard and herself harder. Some bands thrived on laid-back lazing about in the studio; Fire Hazard was more aggressive and tightly strung, they wanted to work hard. They also knew the small budget typically given to a new band had no slack in it for wasteful studio time.

Robbie's work started before the band showed up and continued long after they dragged themselves home. Each day she watched Donal painstakingly set up the studio, then with him she ran over all her notes on the previous day's work. At the end of the evening, which was usually in the small hours of the morning, she took home cassettes of the session to listen to privately.

Once or twice, as she finally crawled into bed at dawn, it crossed her mind that Christy might just be getting up a few doors down the road. Every so often at Emerald she wondered if Chris Lawless, record exec, had spent many hours in a recording studio helping an engineer search for fugitive noises on a thirty-two track tape. For someone so integrally involved in the music world, he neatly managed to avoid *her* part of it; they might have been living on separate continents for all she ran into him. Dublin was a small city, but evidently not that small.

After a week the band had fallen into very professional recording habits; even Donal approved of them. They had learned to balance consistency with the freedom to improvise. Many times during a run-through of a familiar song something sparked and made it new all over again.

During one of these moments, while she sat mesmerized and Donal made minute adjustments on a channel or two, Robbie felt an extra shiver travel up her spine. She ignored it, wary of breaking her concentration. Eamonn's guitar had been building up an emotional head of steam that seemed to erupt into Mairead's final chorus. Robbie unconsciously leaned forward, stiff and tingly, ready for the last measures. Clean and strong, just as she had always heard them in her mind, each instrument closed together in a series of swift, hard notes. Perfect.

The tingle in Robbie's spine did not end with the music; it grew stronger and spread to cover her right shoulder. Before her conscious mind could start to wonder, Christy leaned into her field of vision. With great effort, she did not jump.

His long-fingered hands rested familiarly on the console, obviously at ease among the knobs and levers. His brown arms emerged from the rolled cuffs of a beige suede jacket that was light and supple enough to be a shirt. The soft material called to be touched almost as temptingly as the freshly shaved, honey-gold skin of his cheek.

"They're good," he murmured, still gazing through the glass ahead. Only then did Robbie notice the pride sparkling up from the depths of his eyes. So he hadn't managed to hate rock and roll entirely! It still touched some recess of his shrouded, mysterious heart. Robbie felt as if she had discovered a marvelous secret.

She remarked softly, "Did you doubt it?"

"No. Actually, something kept me from thinking about it at all."

"Something?"

At this, he turned his head to face her. She was caught in a look that seemed like an open door to his soul, but in an instant he had replaced it with his wry smile and slightly abashed explanation, "Maybe the devil was in me." He said it "divil." "I think you have a saying like that in America."

"'The devil made me do it.'"

"Aye. The devil is a busy lad. So, are you well settled in your flat?"

"This follows from a remark about the devil? You really make me wonder, Christy O'Laighleis!"

"Do I now?" He laughed delightedly and took up a careless seat on the console's edge, arms folded across the broad swell of his chest.

Robbie purposely devoted herself to gathering up loose sheets of paper and Styrofoam coffee cups in order to keep from staring at him like an animal caught in a headlight. "To answer your question—yes, I love my flat. Mrs. Hall treats me like a granddaughter and it's very quiet at the back of the house where my bedroom is. I really appreciate your help."

He smiled. "It wasn't a bit of trouble. I had to show you that Irish hospitality wasn't a myth after all, in spite of . . . whatever impression I may have given you."

Her mouth opened to deny that he had given her any but the best impression, but she was mercifully prevented from lying by a sharp rap on the glass before her nose. She looked up to see Mairead gesturing toward the automatic sliding doors that separated studio from booth. Robbie nodded permission and Mairead scuttled over to the switch on her side of the wall.

As the glass panels parted, Christy remarked in admiration, "You've really got her trained!" The next moment he was enveloped in the fierce, half-combative hug of his small sister. He deftly pinned her under one arm and wrestled her to stillness.

She squeaked insults at him. "You murdering savage! It's not enough you make me eat your cooking every night before you let me out of the house! Now you're showing up here to torment me? Did you come to close the place down then?"

"I did," he replied solemnly. "Request by the Minister of the Environment. He says you are *indeed* a hazard."

Her snort of derision suggested how much she cared for opinionated heads of state. "And you? What do you think? Not that I care a penny."

"I'll tell yóu when my head stops ringing from the racket.... Now don't be biting me, girl! I was just getting my thoughts together."

"As if you could! And?"

"And you'll do. You might just do. The singer could use a bit of work but...ouch!" He directed a martyred gaze at Robbie while he hopped on one foot. "Don't ever have a sister—me own's half maimed me."

Robbie couldn't help but laugh at the sight of the squirming girl trapped in Christy's big, gentle arms. "No danger of that—I have no brothers or sisters at all."

Both blondes looked up from their struggle, pity and disbelief plain in their matched, slanting eyes. "Why, that's terrible!" Mairead proclaimed. "All alone in the world! Aw, me ma and da will adopt you. Then you'll at least have *us*."

Robbie thought Mairead was serious for a moment until she heard Christy's stage whisper, "I don't think we've made a good case for ourselves as family, Mairead."

"Oh." She stood up sheepishly, her clothes disordered from pouncing on her brother. "I suppose not. Shall I make adoring eyes at you then?"

"Do you think you could be convincing?"

"No." She sighed. "So what *did* you come down here for if not to praise me and not to make me miserable?"

He shrugged elaborately and his gaze seemed to flick toward Robbie before he could direct it elsewhere. She felt an electric jolt through her body. Nonsense, she told herself, stop imagining hidden meanings in his every move. He's just here because he's curious about the sessions.

"I was just curious," he answered easily, unaware of how exactly he had echoed her thoughts. "All I knew of Fire Hazard was the fearful noise you all used to make in the garage in Howth. I thought I'd see if you had improved." He added with exaggerated reluctance, "Perhaps you have. But it's a great thing you've the sense to hire a good producer. The work she has ahead of her surely boggles the mind, but she might make something of you."

Robbie raked through his statement and his tone for sign of the irony that should be there. It wasn't; he sounded sincere. She busied herself with the console, though there was nothing to do, unsure how to react to this new esteem.

The next thing she heard was his teasing goodbye. "Well, I'm away off— Got to keep the wheels of the empire turning."

"What?" Mairead exclaimed. "No date?"

"Indeed not. I must work every now and again. Tonight I'm up for barbecue with the programming director of our beloved national radio station." He winked at Robbie, causing her heart to skip a beat. "Can you hold off the rain one more night, Robbie?"

She replied with more bravado than she felt, "For Mairead's brother? Of course."

He kissed Mairead and nodded to Robbie. For a terrifying instant she was afraid he would kiss her, too.

Then, after his shining presence was gone from the studio, she wished ardently that he had.

"I can't believe you finished the album in three and a half weeks," Michael murmured.

"That's only the rough tape now. I still have to do the final mix with Donal and then approve the masters."

He waved his hand in a gesture that dismissed this as minor. He and Robbie sat in his little-used office at Lawless Records.

"How long do you figure for the mix-down?"

Robbie had come prepared with an estimate. "Two weeks, three tops."

"Take all the time you need now, you're under budget as it is—unless I'm losing my mind and reading these numbers wrong, which I suspect is the case since I've never heard of someone going *under* budget...." He crossed his eyes comically.

"The band works very clean," Robbie explained with pride. "And Donal Sheehy is a gem."

"Of course it has nothing to do with you."

"Maybe a little."

"All right; well I'll never make the higher-ups believe this financial report, and if I do, they'll never let you leave Ireland, they'll nail you down to a forty-year contract."

She answered without thinking. "If they could guarantee that every record I worked on would be as pleasant an experience as this one has been, they could have me."

Michael laid into her with a serious stare. "We have some good bands, Robbie, and we're out looking for more. You could pretty much have a free hand—make a few discoveries on your own. And it's not a bad sort of a life here at all.''

Flustered, Robbie could only answer his earnestness with a polite evasion. ''I know, Michael. But you know us New Yorkers—you can take the girl out of the city, but you can't take the city out of the girl.'' Even as she said it she had to wonder if it was even true in her case. Could she uproot herself and live in Ireland? The thought was so offbeat she brushed it out of her mind. ''Besides, I already have a tentative commitment to do a movie soundtrack somewhere in France after I leave here.''

''How tentative?''

''Very tentative, but they're holding it open for me until I decide.''

''Ah, well . . . So you said you're thinking of going away for a couple of weeks now?''

''Yup—a real holiday. Someplace different than Dublin, so I can wash all the stale air out of my head and come back fresh to mix the album.''

''Have you thought about where you'll go?''

''I've a few places in mind, nothing firm. Mairead says it's no problem getting one of those bed-and-breakfast places almost everywhere, even this time of year.''

''No, it's not. If you need any help—a car, cash, anything, you'll let me know, won't you?''

''Yes, thank you.'' She knew he made the offer neither as an empty gesture nor one of corporate policy. If she asked, he would cheerfully drive her to the farthest, rockiest corner of the country and put her up with his own aunt. ''Well, must go,'' she said briskly. ''The band is throwing a big 'end of recording' bash at Mairead's parents' house.''

"You've got beautiful weather for it."

"It's been gorgeous since I got here—I think all of you just *say* that Ireland is perpetually rainy in order to keep it to yourselves."

Mairead had promised to line up Christy as Robbie's ride to Howth, but he had regretfully called a few days earlier and said that business would keep him out of Dublin longer than expected; he'd show up at the party *sometime* but Robbie should not wait for him. So she resigned herself to a city bus and was rewarded with a wonderfully scenic ride along the shore of Dublin Bay.

Mairead met her at the bus stop by Howth's harbor and excitedly whisked her into a boxy little car before Robbie had gotten more than a glimpse of the quaint fishing town.

"But, Mairead, I don't get to see fishing boats and lighthouses too often—or smell them. And there's a little island out there...."

"And they've been there for years while me da has only done barbecue twice in recorded history. Take your pick."

"I seem to have taken it.... But you'd better promise me time to explore later. I've got to stock up on all this picturesque stuff before I have to go back to bleak New York."

"I promise!" Mairead crossed her heart, a dangerous gesture considering her casual style of driving. *Bleak* New York? Come on!"

They drove down a sandy, beach-side road to a rambling pink house muffled by masses of rhododendrons and tangled hedge. It was so close to the village Robbie could have walked there in ten minutes; perhaps she really would get a chance to explore later on. Half a

dozen people already dotted the yard; most Robbie
knew as friends of the band. Mairead dragged her happily by the arm into the clean, sunny house and introduced her to her mother.

Mrs. Lawless, a slender, dignified woman who looked
as if she'd be more at home in a law court or on the
floor of the Parliament, smiled up from a huge vat of
potato salad. "Ah, it's grand to meet you, Robbie!"
She shuffled stirring spoons until she could free a hand
to shake Robbie's. Her grip was firm and welcoming.
Robbie saw clearly where her son came by his clear,
strong features and his ease of command. She would
hate to be this woman's adversary—or her son's. The
woman continued, "Can I commandeer your strong,
young arms?"

Even as Robbie smiled assent, Mrs. Lawless handed
her the potato salad.

"And you, Mairead, round up some of the useless
lads and set them to hauling out the lemonade from the
pantry. And take these buns to your da."

Mairead made a face but allowed her mother to pile
her with hot dog and hamburger buns. So far the whole
party was indistinguishable from its counterpart in the
United States, save for the accents of the picnickers.

A flagged patio extended in a broad scallop from the
back of the house, half of it sheltered by a low roof of
weathered timbers. Beneath this a picnic table of the
same driftwood gray already overflowed with the food
and paraphernalia of a feast. Beyond the stone-paved
area spread a lawn as perfect as a bowling green. Micky,
Sean, Eamonn and several girls skirmished across it
with a soccer ball and two enormous dogs.

But all the beauty of the yard and the distracting activity of her friends could not keep Robbie's eyes off the

grander scene beyond. A vast beach, smooth as a length
of velvet, swept down to the lip of the silver-gray sea.
Far out, at the very limit of vision, the water turned a
hazy steel-blue and the horizon blurred into a sky of
leaden clouds.

"Storm coming," Mairead observed at Robbie's side.
"Take it till nightfall to get to us, but I hope Christy's
not fogged in at Heathrow."

"He's in London?"

"Think so, but it's easy to lose track with Christy.
He's on the road so much he's worse than a salesman."

That explained his scarceness during all these weeks
of recording, Robbie decided. She frowned at the on-
coming clouds, willing them to clear a path for Christy's
plane. The desire to see him at home, relaxed for an
entire afternoon, suffused her with a fierce melancholy. Hoping it didn't show in her face, she directed
her frown toward the edge of the yard. "How do you
get down to the beach? It looks like there's a drop."

"About twelve feet worth—it's partly reinforced with
a concrete seawall, and we've rough steps hacked out in
the bank. Go on and look about. We've enough able
bodies to set up the food without you. Me mum was just
doing her sergeant-major act."

"Maybe later. I hate to be antisocial the minute I get
here. Besides, I haven't met your father yet."

"Why, so you haven't. Where is the old dear anyway?"

They found Mr. Lawless in a shade of trees raking up
the fire in a stone barbecue pit. Two dozen enormous
potatoes roasted in the coals. Mairead took after his side
of the family—round of face and elfin. He had frost-
white hair and the bright pink cheeks of someone who

had just run in from the cold. From him poured a warmth as tangible as that of the fire he tended.

"Our guest of honor's here—Ma says lay on a raft of hamburgers," Mairead instructed him.

Robbie asked guiltily, "Was I keeping you from eating? I'm sorry, I would have been here sooner..."

Mr. Lawless grabbed his daughter by a hank of yellow hair and shook her gently. "Don't go upsetting your guest, Mairead! No, no, Robbie, these heathens are *always* hungry—bottomless pits. And they've been stoking themselves with enough crisps and dip to give the entire country of Ireland indigestion. Go on with you now!" He gave Mairead a little shove.

"Crisps" turned out to be potato chips, whereas "chips" were french fries, and "lemonade" was an overall name for soda. Beyond these details, and the fact that the soccer ball was used for Gaelic football— the wildest, roughest game Robbie had ever encountered—the picnic could have passed as American. Robbie laughed and ate and struggled happily through several games of ball.

By midafternoon she had thrown herself under a tree with one wirehaired, pony-size dog to recuperate. A small outburst of greetings back at the house passed unnoticed. It was delicious lying in an ankle-deep sponge of grass with the air on her cheeks and an animal snoozing peacefully beside her. Nothing even remotely similar was possible in New York. There you never closed your eyes and dreamed unless you were locked safely behind stout doors.

Her sense of self-preservation had been lulled by the serenity of this new land; she didn't even look up when she heard the soft rustle of movement and the slow thump-thump of the dog's tail in the grass by her ear.

It took the rumble of a familiar voice to rouse her. "I've been sent out to see if the cooking has killed you."

She opened her eyes and saw above her, dominating the azure sky, the astonishingly tall form of Mairead's brother. In jeans and a blue sweater, his hair tossed about by the wind, he looked as young as any of the frolicking kids, but infinitely more alive and fascinating.

"No, don't get up," he said in response to her sudden scramble. "Rest awhile. It's hard work, all this fresh air and sunshine. I'm sure your city lungs aren't used to it."

"I think they could adjust."

To her happy disbelief he sank down onto the grass beside her and was immediately commandeered as a pillow by the dog. He shushed and patted the animal until it settled with its head in his lap. Within seconds it had fallen asleep as Christy stroked its ears. Robbie fervently envied the creature.

"You weren't fogged in at Heathrow then?"

"No, I invoked your name and the clouds cleared off," he teased.

"So I could get a job in climate control if I wanted to stay in Ireland?"

"Undoubtedly. But you wouldn't stay, I think."

"Why not? I like it here."

"Of course you do. Everyone likes it here on their holidays. Then they go back to wherever they're from and are quite happy with their photo albums and Aran-knit jumpers."

"Jumpers?"

"Sweaters you call them—like this," he pulled the soft aqua blue wool away from his flat stomach in illustration.

"Well, I haven't taken any photos or bought any sweaters. And besides that, I'm not even here on holiday, so maybe I don't come under your sweeping generalization, Mr. Irish Tourist Board."

Surprised out of his confident observations, he looked down at her through sharp eyes. "You *will* be different, won't you?"

"You make it sound like a crusade on my part," she said, laughing. "I'm really an incorrigibly lazy slob. There's only one thing I work at."

"Your career."

"Right."

"And that's why you'll never move to Ireland."

"Ugh." She groaned. "I'll go crazy arguing with you. Lie down and shut up."

He did most readily and Robbie soaked in the wine of his presence until she felt drunk with it. One could make a life of this, she decided. "*If* one never had to totally wake up and face the differences of goal and temperament that separated them...."

Smack into the middle of her reverie came the thud of a soccer ball. She jerked alert in time to hear the surprised yelp of the dog, which had scrambled to its feet, and to see Christy snatch the ball before its second bounce. Eamonn yelled from the far side of the yard, "Come on, old man! Give us our ball back or play!"

A look of merry determination peeled a few more years off Christy's face until Robbie had the distinct impression she was looking at the little boy inside him. In one graceful motion he trapped the ball between his

S♥I♥L♥H♥O♥U♥E♥T♥T♥E

LUCKY HEARTS

SWEEPSTAKES

GRAND PRIZE

Cruise the World

on the

QE2

OR CHOOSE
$100,000.00
CASH!

Global tour for 2 on the world's most luxurious ship. Dance, dine, see romantic ports, ancient civilizations, elegant cities—a lifetime of memories!

Over 200 prizes! More to win...see inside

Enter a new world of ROMANCE...FREE PRIZES.
No purchase necessary to enter and win!

4 FIRST PRIZES
Pearls from the Orient. Win a strand of the world's most beautiful treasures—earrings to match.

10 SECOND PRIZES
Bask in the Bermuda Sun. Take a long, romantic weekend for 2.

25 THIRD PRIZES
5-Piece Luggage Set. Lightweight and durable for stylish adventures—anywhere!

200 FOURTH PRIZES
$25.00 Cash. Buy yourself a gift in any store in the country—on us!

SILHOUETTE SPECIAL INTRODUCTORY OFFE

4 SILHOUETTE ROMANCE novels FREE, a $7.80 value. Lose yourself in the timeless drama of love played out in locations the world over.

FREE FOLDING UMBRELLA, just for accepting 4 FREE BOOKS with this introductory offer.

FREE EXTRAS: Our monthly Silhouette Books Newsletter... a Mystery Gift Bonus.

FREE HOME DELIVERY. We'll then send brand-new books each month, as soon as the are published, to examine FREE for 15 days. Pay just $11.70—that's it. No shipping, ha dling or other charge. Cancel anytime yo wish. The 4 FREE BOOKS AND UMBRELLA a yours to keep.

GET 4 FREE BOOKS, FREE FOLDING UMBRELLA, FREE MYSTERY GIFT!

TO ENTER: Fill out, detach below, and affix postage. See back pages of books for OFFICIAL SWEEPSTAKES INFORMATION and mail your entry before deadline date shown in rules.

S♥I♥L♥H♥O♥U♥E♥T♥T♥E
LUCKY HEARTS
SWEEPSTAKES

Free prizes—you must enter to win. Detach here and mail today!

Sweeps entry—process immediately!

Silhouette Books®

Prize Headquarters
120 Brighton Road
P.O. Box 5084
Clifton, NJ 07015-5084

feet, pulled off his sweater, which he threw to Robbie, scooped up the ball again and sprang into the game.

As far as Robbie was concerned, he couldn't have done anything to cause her more intense discomfort. The sight of him among all those scrawny adolescents, his chest and arms as hot and fluid as molten gold, quite undid her. She pulled the sweater right side out and took it into the kitchen.

Mrs. Lawless had just set a stack of pans in the sink.

"May I help you wash up?"

"No, love, these'll soak for a while. But I can put you to work shelling walnuts, if you like."

"Sure! I'm desperately afraid of getting shanghaied into another game of football. I make a total fool of myself at sports."

The older woman chuckled as she set a bowl of nuts and a steel cracker before Robbie. "That's half the reason I stay in here with the food. That and the fact that there's no end to the amount these kids can eat, bless them."

"It does seem like feeding an army."

"It is indeed. True, I never had more than two of them at home at one time—there's nine years between Chris and Rosie, and another six on down to Mairead—but you never saw children with such a gang of starving friends!"

Robbie contentedly cracked nuts and listened to Mrs. Lawless reminisce about raising children. It sounded so cozy and safe growing up in Ireland, even on the fringes of Dublin. Robbie's own childhood, though happy, had been spent on concrete. She had never thought seriously about having children before, but she thought now that Ireland would be far more healthy and nurturing an environment for them than New York.

Chapter Six

Do I hear people bandying my name about?" Christy ambled into the kitchen, shirtless and glowing from exertion. He planted a kiss on his mother's cheek while Robbie struggled to attend to her walnuts.

"Ach, you're sweaty as a racehorse, get away with you!" Mrs. Lawless complained.

"I'm just coming in to take a quick shower. And then I'm rescuing this poor American from your food factory."

Robbie looked up.

Christy's eyes twinkled at her. "Mairead said you were interested in exploring a bit. I've been living away for a while but I won't get us lost on the strand—or on the beach, as you call it."

"Oh," she said inadequately. "Thank you."

"Stay put then." He hugged his mother again over her protests and propelled himself out of the kitchen.

Robbie's head whirled. Why was he being so nice? Did he feel a duty to be a good host simply because this was a Lawless party and he was a Lawless? Before she settled on a comforting answer, he reappeared damp and freshly clad in threadbare white painter's pants and a white shirt under a crimson sweater. He looked like an ad out of a men's fashion magazine. And Mairead complained that his taste in clothing had *deteriorated*.

"Have you a jacket, Robbie?" he asked, slipping his sockless feet into sneakers. "There's a fair breeze blowing in from that storm."

She grabbed the denim jacket from the back of her chair and obediently put it on while hurrying through the door he held for her. The amateur athletes outside had collapsed in various heaps all over the patio. Christy nudged Mairead with his foot. "Anyone for a walk on the beach?"

"Argh," she groaned, burying her face in her arms.

Christy bent over to gloat in her ear, "You're a sorry specimen, Lalor. How do you expect to survive three months on the road as a rock star, eh?"

She replied miserably, "Drugs."

Robbie gasped in horror. "Mairead!"

The girl looked up sheepishly. "Vitamins?" Then she hid again and said, "Ah, lay off, the two of you— touring can't be half as murderous as Gaelic football."

Christy's laugh convinced Robbie that he hadn't taken his sister's remarks too seriously. She shouldn't have either; she was just extrasensitive to Christy's disapproval. She had met no one since Simon who could so unnerve her with a look or a gesture, and Simon himself seemed like a dull precursor of this man, tarnished brass next to genuine gold. As she accepted his hand down the steep, uneven steps to the seawall, she was shaken to feel the hot surge of life through his flesh. It was hardly fair that she should be brought into such close contact with a man who, no matter how he had learned to tolerate her for his sister's sake, could never wholeheartedly approve of her.

"Do you want to walk along the seawall or on the sand?"

His question gave her an excuse to keep her eyes off him. She kicked off her shoes and bent over to gather them up. "The sand."

"You'll freeze your feet."

"You must think I'm a hopeless sissy, Mr. O'Laighleis," she complained archly and jumped the two feet to the wet sand. It was indeed cold, but so hard she didn't sink in. Christy followed her, one eyebrow and one corner of his mouth raised thoughtfully.

The strand at low tide was a hundred yards wide and stretched nearly half a mile in each direction. Robbie headed toward the harbor though she had no idea if the beach extended that far. About a mile out in the water rose the rocky little bump of island that she had seen when the bus let her off in Howth.

"What's that island?" she asked.

"It's called Ireland's Eye. I used to go out there as a boy and sit with the gulls. It's only a short way off-shore but somehow you get a whole new perspective out there. Anyway, that tower—you can just make it out—looks due west about sixty miles to Anglesey in Wales."

"Sixty miles? My gosh, you *are* close to Great Britain."

"Closer and closer all the time," he murmured regretfully.

She stole a glance at his averted face and wondered at the sad expression there. "What is it about Ireland that's so special to you, Christy?" she asked timidly.

"I don't know...that sounds half-witted, doesn't it? But that's the problem—we no longer know what makes us special, we just have this vague feeling that being Irish means something... Well, some don't even have that, I'm afraid. From the day they're born they look across one sea or another for their values and life-styles. You can't blame them; we haven't bothered to keep anything native alive, except a bit of music and dancing that hasn't changed for generations.

"Kids can't relate to that, they don't feel they've had any part in making it. A culture has got to grow and develop in order to stay valid to people." He shook himself, seeming almost to come out of a dream. "I'm sorry—you don't need a sociology lecture."

"I'd like to understand though. I only recently learned of the history of Lawless Records."

"Hmm..." he began speculatively. The melancholy in his sweet face lifted in favor of humor. "I don't know whether to thank Michael Shaw for that or kill him. He's a good man though. I'm glad he's handling Mairead's band."

Though Robbie managed to make no sound, her surprised look caught his attention.

"Did you think I loathed everything she's doing and everyone she's associated with?"

"Well, uh..."

"I guess that shouldn't surprise me. No, my oppressive overprotectiveness of my baby sister is not political. She could sing Italian opera if she wanted, or Indian mantras, whatever made her happy. She doesn't have to be 'Irish' to please me."

Robbie waited for him to go on. They had wandered far down the beach out of sight of the house, hopping on and off the seawall as it suited them. Her feet were not callused enough for the crumbling concrete, she knew she'd be in agony as soon as they thawed out. But she wouldn't have interrupted Christy for any reason short of death. He was giving her a glimpse into his soul—a glimpse that would doubtless do her no good. Had he been simply another beautiful-looking man she would have eventually been able to get over him. But men with sensitive, complex souls were not so forgettable.

"How long have you been in rock, Robbie?"

"Five years—five years getting paid, that is."

"So long? I spent less time with Lawless before giving up on it."

"Well, my job's not very glamorous, so no one puts pressure on me like they put on you."

He gave her an incredulous look. "Not glamorous? Producers are more stars than the musicians sometimes. Look at Simon Beyer."

"I am *not* Simon Beyer." She was afraid she sounded a little more cross than she had intended.

"You could be if you wanted. There's nothing separating you from that sort of infamy but your own integrity—which I did not acknowledge at first and for that I beg your pardon."

She shrugged self-consciously.

"But you've seen that Mairead is a bit, well . . ."

"Star-struck."

"That'll do. When I ran Lawless I lost some of my acts to the major labels. We didn't offer what I suppose you might call fringe benefits.'"

She knew what he meant—a fast life-style, pampering, drugs, women...

"I know she eventually always comes around to sense, but in some things the first mistake is the decisive one. I'd like her to be with people who don't push her into those things. She thinks I'm trying to take the choice away from her, but I don't think she really sees how *bad* it can be."

Robbie thought carefully before she replied. She no longer feared that he'd explode in temper, but she didn't know how much advice he'd accept from her as an outsider. "You *have* to let people make their own decisions, even if they seem to be teetering on the edge of a cliff."

"Ach, I know! That's the basis of all the work I'm doing now, in fact, letting kids determine their own radio programming. But somehow it's a different story with your own flesh and blood. It's harder.... Mairead says *you* grew up in a rough area of New York. Yet here you are, neither a junkie nor a criminal. How did you turn out so well?"

She curtsied elaborately. "Thank you for noticing, kind sir. Seriously, though—I made plenty of mistakes. The worst of them had nothing in particular to do with rock exactly." She trailed off, her face clouding at the memory.

"Can you tell me what this dreadful mistake was?"

She groaned in self-disgust. "Love."

"Ah yes, that can indeed turn your head inside out...."

Mairead had claimed her brother had determinedly avoided romance for this very reason, so she felt it fairly safe to tease him. "I expect *you* turned the heads of a lot of innocent young girls when you were a hotshot record exec.''

However lightly she had meant this, he responded with a pensive sigh. "If I turned the heads of any innocents this is the first I've heard of it.''

Seeking to coax his humor back she pressed onward. "What? Weren't you inundated with women? I've never known a rock man in a position of power who wasn't courted constantly.''

"Ah, but not by *innocents*.''

The truth of his implication shut her up. Of course the women he met wouldn't have been sweet, naive girls. They would have been ambitious, worldly-wise women who knew how to manipulate their way up through the rock and roll hierarchy, and were neither romantic nor scrupulous about how they did it.

"Well,'' she said after a few thoughtful moments. "I can see why you never married.''

Suddenly his smile returned. "Oh, it's worse than that. In Ireland marriage is one of those choices for which you get no second chances.''

"Why is that?''

"Divorce is illegal.''

"You're kidding!''

"I'm not—it's proscribed by the constitution itself.''

"Wow...they're really serious, aren't they?''

"So you see, if you're a fearful coward such as myself, the law drives you into bad habits with the women, I'm afraid.''

She didn't want to ask what these bad habits might be, she could imagine. Her head was filled with speculations about Helena and Aideen and Peggy...and an unknown quantity of others.

"And what nice Irish girl would take a chance on a suspect creature like myself anyway?"

Any Irish girl who was not a fool, she wanted to say, but two circumstances prevented her—circumspection and a sharp stone that stuck up from the concrete. It stabbed her foot, she yelped and toppled directly onto Christy. His arms went around her and his strong, young body, sturdy as the trunk of a tree, became her ground, her whole world of support. Ever so slowly he let her slide down his stomach until her toes touched the ground; his eyes were filled with such perplexed emotion she was afraid to look into them, afraid she could read whatever she wanted in their darkness. Her fingertips pressed tenuously against his chest and felt the accelerated beat of his heart, his shallow, irregular breathing. When he found his voice it rasped from some unfathomable depth. "This is one of my bad habits," he said.

Then he nestled her head back into the curve of his arm and lowered his head. His lips met hers in the most delicate of passions, touching her as one would stroke the cheek of a sleeping child. Everything about him was a caress: his warm breath on her face, his low, soothing sigh, the pulse of his wrist at her nape, the way he rocked her slowly onto his hips.

It was their first kiss in anything like friendship and it devastated her. Her mind went soft and fuzzy as a cloud, her body obeyed a long-dormant will, without volition she unfolded to the touch of his body, thigh to thigh, belly to belly, heat fusing with heat. When his kiss deepened and erased the boundaries of their flesh she was not shocked. He tasted like fire and life itself. Her last thought, before thought evaded all control, was that she had slipped from her old, solid world into a fresh, new one that had been created the very moment she fell into Christy's arms.

Then those arms dragged her away. The pain of the separation wrenched a cry from her and she clutched Christy's neck, dizzy and confused.

"I'm sorry," he said raggedly.

She couldn't speak, but her every breath was itself a hoarse reply. She felt as if she might explode with anger or even shame. He was *sorry*?

He took her head between gentle hands and forced her to look up at him. When she did, her anger died; he looked as ravaged as she felt, strained and stunned. "I had no intentions of... I'm sorry."

This time she managed to squeeze out a few words. "This is one of your bad habits?"

"No... *no* ... Worse than that." His anguished gaze dropped from her face and he whispered, "I... I think I was leading us into one of those mistakes... that you can never correct."

"I see," she choked out.

His fingers skimmed down her shoulders and arms and grasped her hands lightly. He was still looking down at the cold sand. "We'd best go back."

She pulled away, breaking even that minimal contact between them. "You go. I'll be along later. If anyone asks, tell them I wanted to do a little exploring on my own...."

His last look was one of inarticulate pleading. For forgiveness? For another chance? For what? She knew she'd fall apart if she had to bear it another second, so she turned smartly and struck off down the empty strand. When next she looked back she could just see Christy's broad form halfway back to the house, a spot of red as bright as blood.

Christy had to shake himself several times before he could face the cheerful crowd back at the house. He waved as he sprang energetically up the steps from the beach; perhaps any peculiar look that lingered about his face could be passed off as exertion.

Mairead called accusingly from the patio, "And what have you done with Robbie, pray tell? Have you left her drowned?"

His heart lurched sickeningly against his ribs—then he made himself remember that this was a perfectly normal question for her to ask since he *had* returned alone. He strode up the lawn willing his mouth to recite the story Robbie had given him to tell. "Well, I see now where your sympathies lie, and it's not with your poor aged brother. Robbie's still off exploring, while I, if it's of any concern to your hard heart, am dead with exhaustion."

"Fa!" she discounted his remark shortly. "My heart's breaking for you. So don't be standing there teetering on your two legs if you're knackered, sit down."

That he could not do, not here in front of all these eyes, though none but Mairead's were curious. "No, I brought work with me. I'm due in Kerry in a few days and I have quite a bit more to do on that project. You juveniles have permission to continue the party without me."

"As if we're needing it!" she yelled after him, deftly hitting him between the shoulder blades with a sponge-rubber ball.

Once inside the house his control slipped and his brows squeezed together in pain. Too soon. His mother stood at the range stirring a pot of chocolate sauce. "Why, Christy love, is your head aching?"

He straightened his face abruptly. "A bit. The glare off the water, I suppose. I think I'll go upstairs and lie down a while."

"Well, your room's always ready for you."

"I know, Mam." He cast her a grateful smile.

"Will you be down for ice cream later? It's walnut chocolate chip. Poor Robbie just about broke her hands cracking the nuts for it."

"I don't know. Don't hold anyone up for me."

Only when he reached the old familiar sanctum of his boyhood room and closed the door did he let his misery drive to the surface. He gripped the edge of his old desk until his knuckles turned white and he squeezed his eyes shut with a desperate resolve, but he could not erase the heartbreaking image of Robbie's lovely face as she had gazed up at him in confusion. He could have taken his skull and crushed it between his own two hands, he was that furious. Certainly there'd be no brain inside it to harm. He knew no name foul enough to call himself. He had lived for years according to a rigid set of rules that made sense to the cynic he had become. And today he had broken them as if they meant less than nothing.

For how many weeks had he known he was falling in love with this impossibly sweet American? Four? Since she had brought Mairead home drunk and had defied him with her nonexistent wickedness? Every touch of her skin, every sight of her unassuming beauty had proved the stupidity of his arrogance. Oh, he had been so sure that he had the world all figured out! Years of Helenas and Peggys—women who were beautiful yet uninspiring—had convinced him that there *were* no other sorts of women, certainly not in the world he had given up but which still held his heart. Thus he had felt quite safe and had congratulated himself on his masterful control of destiny. All around him friends and foes alike made rash and foolish decisions based on the vagaries of love. He never needed to question his own decisions, he was always one step clear of such reckless emotion. He would never fall in love; it was as simple as that.

Except that he *had* fallen in love—with a woman who would no sooner sink into the bogs of Ireland with him than she would drive nails through her eardrums. *He* had given up rock, at what emotional cost he could not admit, but it would be insane to expect the same of her. He knew from his remaining contacts in the industry that Robbie was on the verge of major success. Despite her modesty, she was one of the high-magnitude stars in her field. In London Christy had even had the misfortune to run into Simon Beyer at a party and endure his pumped-up boasting that *he* had discovered and made Robbie Calderón himself. From what Christy knew of the vainglorious, lazy Beyer, Robbie had developed *in spite of* his help.

But no matter how Robbie had arrived at her present eminence, Christy O'Laighleis, civil servant, had no right to even fantasize about asking her to give it up. And he could not play with her as he played with women who knew they were involved in a game. Robbie was reality, a reality he could not afford to lay hands on.

But he *had* laid his hands on her. Now what should he do?

At the knock upon his door he opened his mouth to snarl out a curt dismissal. Mairead walked in before the first syllable. She wore one of her "I may be younger but I'm a woman and therefore wiser" looks. He tensed; he had never quite learned how to overwhelm her with the force of masculine logic.

"You told me you'd be working, you told ma you'd be lying down. Now I find you staring at a snag in the rug looking simpleminded."

"Perhaps I'm casting about for inspiration."

"You're casting about for your *marbles*, brother mine. Everyone else in this house may have eaten themselves into a coma, but *I've* me two eyes in straight. Perhaps you can tell me why Robbie came back from her walk seven shades whiter than when she left."

He didn't hide his jerk of reaction quickly enough. Mairead narrowed her cat's eyes and said, "Aha!" As she closed in, Christy pivoted away. She cornered him between the desk and the windowsill. Feeling ridiculous, he gave up the fight. She grabbed two handfuls of his hair and anchored his head so he could not evade her scrutiny. Their eyes were very alike; she could read him as she would a mirror. "You're in love with her, aren't you, Christy O'Laighleis?"

"Now, Mairead," he began. "Don't let your fancy run away with you...."

"Oh shut up, don't waste your talk on *me*. I've been waiting *years* to see you at the mercy of something you couldn't control. Let me enjoy it."

"Mairead..."

"The question is—are you man enough to tell her? Or are you going to let her get sucked back to New York when we want her *here* with *us*?"

This was something he could answer. "She *is* going back to New York, Mairead. Face the facts."

His sister glared at him with disgust plain in every sharp feature. Her hands curled into small fists and hung impotently at her sides. Before she turned away she pronounced her verdict on him. "Coward."

Robbie spent a good half hour on the strand staring at the little island called Ireland's Eye and wishing she were on it, before she prepared herself to face the party. She couldn't decide whether it was a relief or an anticlimax that Christy remained upstairs for the rest of the evening. She ate the homemade ice cream, sipped whiskey with the family after the other guests had left, all the while feeling as if her skin must be made of glass and all her hurts visible. True, neither Mr. nor Mrs. Lawless gave her any cause for this paranoia but something about Mairead's extra-kind familiarity disconcerted her. In addition a dull nervousness gummed up her brain. She could get no distance from her turbulent emotions; she had the claustrophobic impression of being at the bottom of a dark and collapsing well.

The chance to escape, even though it was only to Rose's old room for the night, gave Robbie a great sense of relief, until she realized that the room next to hers belonged to Christy and that the occasional small sounds she heard were his. Since the walk on the beach she had felt inexplicably linked to him; every footfall or scrape of a chair on the floor brought images to her mind as vivid as physical experience. At one point, as she sat on the broad windowsill and watched the sun sink behind a purple, storm-clotted horizon, she thought she heard someone stop outside her door. Her heart itself stopped for the long moments before the someone moved on.

And they said *women* were moody! Christy would make the flightiest woman seem as cut-and-dried as figures in a ledger. His reactions ricocheted all over the realm of possibility like loose bullets. If he had *planned* to unhinge her he could not have done a better job. He was friendly, he was cold; he warned her off Mairead, he commended her for her good influence; he found her a flat, then he seemed to drop off the face of the earth; he lectured her, he confided his heart; he kissed her in cruelty, then kissed her in what bore a strong resemblance to love.

Then again, what did she know about men? Robbie asked herself. For the first time this lack of experience seemed to her a problem. She had known very few men as more than friends—a few mild teenage crushes, and then Simon. Ignorant as she was, she knew enough not to try to measure Christy by Simon's rule. She was utterly adrift. *That* at least fit perfectly with her previous experience—her emotions invariably led her into chaos.

The next morning Robbie's face bore the marks of a strained night. Fortunately the storm had finally beaten its way across the Irish Sea and spent hours pummeling the coast like a berserk drummer—thunder, wind as solid as the crash of a giant's fist, but no rain. Had the night been still, Robbie would have laid in a sweat listening for every whisper of movement in the room next door.

Mairead thoughtfully brought a pot of coffee out to her on the patio and offered an extra sweater.

"What do you mean you're not cold? I've never heard of a foreigner who didn't gripe about the wicked damp of Ireland on their two weeks over here."

"I thought every foreigner who ever set foot in Ireland loved it."

"Oh they *do*. I'm not *explaining* them, just reporting on their curious behavior."

"I see," Robbie replied with a fairly convincing smile. The night had pushed the mess with Christy a short way back into the past. She no longer felt as if the problem sat right on the top of her skull. But it was up there somewhere and needed only the appearance of Christy himself to drop.

"So, where is everybody?" she asked warily.

Mairead answered in detail. "Me mum's gone off to hospital to visit one of her cronies. Da's in town trying to get some fresh fish for supper. And Christy is away off saving the youth of the nation through the airwaves."

"He certainly *does* go on a lot of business trips."

Mairead wrinkled her short nose. "I suppose you could call them that. But it seems a bit of a grand name for hopping about through the bogs of Ireland. Now *Paris*, I'd call that a business trip worth the name. New York, Tokyo... Ah, the names even *taste* good. Well, on the subject of exotic places, have you decided where you'll be spending your holiday away from Fire Hazard?"

Robbie sighed. This morning the idea of a holiday struck her as meaningless; she might as well stay in Dublin, or go back to New York for that matter. There was no way she could clear her mind of Christy. "Gosh, Mairead, I have no idea. Someplace that's all scenery and no people, I suppose. But that sounds like half of Ireland."

"More than half."

"You could just put me on a train and have the conductor dump me someplace. Why don't you just pick a town?"

"You're so hard to please! All right then—our clan is quite partial to Kerry."

"Okay, when do I leave?"

Her young friend frowned at such casualness. "Well, Kerry is rather a big place, as places go in Ireland. It's a whole country—like one of your states, I suppose. We've camped all over but I'm thinking you'd like a little bit more comfort, so I suggest a village called Dunquin on the Dingle Peninsula. You can rent a wee cottage right on the slopes overlooking the ocean."

"As long as it's quiet and private."

"Oh it's private, all right. It's almost literally the ends of the earth—the Blasket islands right off the coast there are the westernmost points of land in Europe."

"I'm sold."

Mairead had not exaggerated a bit about the scenic wonder of the Dingle Peninsula. If the landscape wasn't one of steep, velvet green, sheep-dotted meadows or ferny forests, it was cliffs of black granite that plunged into the thundering, steel-blue Atlantic. New York seemed centuries away, as if North America had yet to be discovered.

Her landlady, Mrs. Foley, a stout woman in Wellingtons and a very serious rubber raincoat, picked her up in the town of Dingle proper and drove her out to Dunquin on a road that made a cow path look like a super highway. While Robbie clutched the sides of her seat in alarm, Mrs. Foley kept up a nonstop critique of the passing scene, the ineptness of the government, the cost of living and the summer's unusually fine weather. Robbie had to struggle to understand her thick, tarry brogue; it was almost as burred as a Scot's. It sounded as if the Kerry manner of speech had grown from the rough landscape itself. The delicate Dublin accent, the lilt that sang like music from Christy's lips, might have come from a different country entirely.

"Will you be renting a car while you're here?" Mrs. Foley wanted to know.

"No, I thought I'd walk or cycle. I'm not sure I trust myself driving these roads—on the right-hand side of the car, no less."

"Why, you'd pick it up in no time. But we've bicycles going to waste up at the cottages and you're young and strong. You might just make the hills. It's a bit of a ride around Slea Head."

Typical Irish understatement, Robbie commented to herself as they climbed an endless hill through blackberry-hedged pastures. Finally they emerged onto a skinny ribbon of road that girdled the promontory called Slea Head and she saw that the beautiful view of cliff and strand would be worth any ride.

"My God, is that a ship?"

"Aye, Spanish freighter. It was driven onto the rocks during a storm three or four years ago. We have some great storms. The strand is lovely for a walk when it's calm, though the water could freeze the legs off you. And there's an even more sheltered cove right up by the cottages."

The cottages proved to be little whitewashed houses with slate roofs; they glittered like bright toys in the late afternoon sunshine. Mrs. Foley launched into her hostess pitch. "At the inn we've a dining room if you don't like to cook, and a parlor where the guests can mingle—you're the only one currently, but we're expecting a lovely man in a couple of days. I've put a few supplies in your kitchen so you can make a snack for yourself, but every morning either I or my daughter Mary drives into Dingle to do errands and get the newspapers. You're welcome to run in any time you like. There's great shopping in Dingle—and a cinema as well. Here you are now. I'll just come in and show you the quirks of the place."

The tiny cottage managed to offer a bedroom, a snug living room with a stone fireplace, a delightfully modern bath and a minuscule kitchen that suited Robbie's minimal culinary skills. An electric kettle for coffee and a knife to spread peanut butter would have sufficed; she intended to take all her meals at the inn.

The lack of neighbors also suited her, she wanted company even less than she wanted a kitchen. The bare cliffs and empty beaches soothed her, she felt she could sit on a rock and stare at the lacy waves for the entire two weeks.

As Mrs. Foley bustled toward the door to leave she stopped and turned to Robbie with a puzzled expression on her face. "Oh, Lord save us—I nearly forgot! You had a phone call even before your bus arrived. It was a Michael Shaw. He left a message—I hope you can make sense if it, it meant nothing to me."

"What did he say?"

"That Two Time just went platinum."

"Yes, I understand it."

"Good. Well, ta then."

Robbie stood beside her unopened suitcase considering Michael's message. The album she had done for Two Time had just sold one million units. Why didn't she feel thrilled?

Two days later the thrill had still failed to hit her. Every morning she had coffee and soft-boiled eggs in the cozy inn, then she took Mrs. Foley's packed lunch and set off for a day in the biting spray at Slea Head.

Though she always took a book with her it usually stayed in her backpack, ignored for the more mysterious stories her mind wove from the sounds of wave and gull. She felt scoured clean by the peace of this place that cared nothing for human beings. She knew she'd go back to the mixing of Fire Hazard's album with her mind washed clear of all its stale musical notions

She only wished she could be so easily rid of her other notions. Though she passed blissful hours with no thought in her head but wonder at the beauty around her, Robbie knew that misery lurked just below the surface. Love for Christy had sunk deep into her bones, beyond the reach of any vacation to erase.

The third morning, through the salt-spattered window of the inn, she noticed Mary Foley take a pile of linen out to one of the empty cottages and remembered with displeasure that another guest had been foretold. How possessive she had become of this corner of the world! She decided to take one of the bikes for a long, thorough pedal around the peninsula. It was over twelve miles into Dingle, so she ought to keep quite busy for most of the day and avoid having to be sociable with the new guest.

Chapter Seven

The ride to Dingle seemed to be eighty percent down-hill, which meant, of course, that the return would be eighty percent *uphill*. Robbie fortified herself in town with a good seafood lunch, a bottle of Guinness and a quiet stroll along the dock past the piles of orange fishing nets. When she thought she felt rested enough she mounted Mrs. Foley's ten-speed and pushed herself down the road. She knew she'd be sore the next day, but the fresh, cold air gave her the vigor to enjoy every mile...at least until the last long hill up to the broken cliffs. The hedges that bordered the road and the fields were old embankments of stone and dirt, woven together over a hundred years by tough blackberry bush. Often rising over her head, they broke the wind for most of the uphill trek. But right at the summit, where the road curved out onto open cliff, they fell away and the wind roared in full force from the open Atlantic.

Though the sky shone blue and storm free, the wind pushed Robbie to a wobbly standstill before she made it around the turn. Tired from the climb, she gave up and resigned herself to walking the bike for a couple of miles. She got off, took hold of the handlebars and pushed forward. Just as she began to clear the shelter of the hedges the wind, roaring and shrill, smacked her like a hand, lifted the bike right out of her grasp and carried it skittering over the blacktop for ten or fifteen feet.

Robbie had never seen such a thing. She stared at the bike in amazement. Then she dragged it upright and set off again, gripping it fiercely. Her hair stung her face like hundreds of tiny whips, the thunder of the wind grew in her ears until she couldn't even hear her own grumbled comments. She made progress for a few steps and then floundered. It was all she could do to stay in one spot, leaning forward against a virtual wall of air.

She backed off and stood awhile in consternation. Frustration and tiredness bubbled out of her as giddy laughter and she leaned back against the hedge giggling uncontrollably. She had never before been physically stopped by nature. Even the worst blizzards in New York had been negotiable. Yet here she stood in bright, placid sunshine, unable to walk on an open road. The experience was novel enough to be fun, though she had no clear idea how to get home. She supposed she'd have to coast down the hill and either find a ride to Dunquin or another road. She wondered about the choice; there weren't too many cars in this part of the world, or too many roads.

She didn't notice the car until it stopped three feet from her rear wheel—a red sports car with its roof up. The sight of the tall, broad-shouldered man who hopped out and hesitated by the side of it startled the laughter right out of her. The wind ripped his name from her mouth. "Christy!"

Careless of any traffic, he recovered from his own immobility and strode determinedly over to her side of the road. "Don't tell me," he yelled. "My sister sent you here, didn't she?"

Robbie nodded, puzzled. "What are *you* doing here?"

"Business, as of course she knew. Get in the car, I'll strap your bike across the trunk and take you back to Mrs. Foley's."

Despite the jolt of pleasure that his appearance had caused her, Robbie had no desire to squeeze into a tiny car with him. She would have pedaled all the way back to Dingle to avoid it. Just standing there looking at his beloved face twisted her insides into knots. "How do you know where I'm staying?"

One of his short, abrupt eyebrows rose. "Where else would Mairead put you? The Lawlesses always stay with Mrs. Foley."

Casting about for a better excuse, she tried to sound blithe about her predicament. "Oh, thanks anyway, but I don't mind riding the rest of the way. I'm sure it won't be bad once I get around Slea Head."

His expression grew unarguably stern. "You won't *get* around Slea Head on a bike. We won't even get around it in my car. I'm going to have to go back to Ventry and take the north road. And if you don't want some amateur doing the final mix on Mairead's album, you'll ride with me."

As if to press home Christy's point, an extra-strong blast of wind knocked Robbie onto her handlebars. Christy's hand shot out and steadied the bike before it fell over with her. She made a desperate face that she hoped her whipping hair would disguise, looked up into his carefully serious eyes and nodded.

Over these roads with their sudden, roller-coaster turns, Christy drove much more recklessly than he ever had in Dublin. Robbie held herself still on the passenger's side. She hadn't yet decided whether to talk to him or pass the ride in silence. Talking to him would have required looking at him, and she wasn't sure she could handle that. The wind had whipped his hair back into honey-colored ripples, and stung his cheeks pink. His Portuguese tan was fading; he would look very Irish when he was again as pale as Mairead. His clothes suited the wild countryside perfectly—a heather-tweed blazer over a cream-white fisherman's sweater. The sports car remained an odd touch in this rugged landscape, but she supposed it was no more incongruous than the neat, white radar antennae that turned atop the old fishing boats in Dingle harbor.

What *was* out of place here was the constraint she felt between them. She knew how she would act toward him if he gave her the chance—all her customary caution would slip from her, shrugged off like an overcoat in order to feel the invigorating bite of wind and sun. Her love for Simon had not fitted her for this love. The earlier infatuation had been for a symbol of rock, not for a man. The woman in Christy's arms had felt this difference in every newly awakened fiber of her body. She had been stripped back to a basic response, one wiser than consciousness, and more demanding.

She knew that she had been born for Christy; her mouth had been formed to the shape of his name and his tongue; her skin had been spangled with nerves to feel every fascinating texture of his, every deep pulse of bloods, every contour of muscle and bone, his heat, his breath.

Even sitting apart like this in a car, she felt as if her body had softened like clay worked by a potter's hands, and the slightest touch from Christy could mold her any way he desired.

He was the one who finally broke the silence with a safe question. "Are you enjoying Kerry?"

"It's fabulous. Being a city girl I've never seen anything like this." A safe answer. Unoriginal as the exchange had been, Robbie felt her mind grinding as furiously as the gears of the car, trying to propel the conversation down the least painful channels.

"I'd think you'd be bored. It's a quiet life."

"That's what I came for. I've really enjoyed wandering around and thinking my thoughts." She bit her tongue—that last was quite untrue. Her thoughts had been grueling. "I don't mean that I'd turn down the chance to *do* something. I've seen notices for dances and stuff posted in Dingle, but I'm not quite bold enough to impose myself on the local people. I expect they have enough of tourists during the season." The burst of light chatter had emptied her reservoir. "What is your business here?"

"I've been working with a group of kids—teenagers who started about a year ago petitioning for more airplay for their local bands. Their letters impressed someone somewhere in the government and their requests were sent to me. I came out and have been helping them with an idea they have for their own program. We've just about worked out all the details. Tonight is the final meeting, tomorrow is the first broadcast."

"That sounds wonderful!" she declared enthusiastically. "Boy, I wish *I* had had a chance to do something like that as a kid. It surprises people to hear this, but for the past several years in New York, radio has *stunk*!"

A small but genuine grin lit his face. "Why don't you come with me then? I was just on my way to the meeting. You could take our ideas back to the States with you—it's about time we started exporting our culture to *you* instead of the other way around."

"You know, I really should...."

"Should?"

"I *will*. Next time I'm pushing some record with one of those aggravating programming directors on WETT or some other wimpy station, I'll enjoy saying, 'Well, in *Ireland* they do it this way....'"

A tall transmitting tower was the only thing that set off the radio station from the other low white buildings that dappled the area to which Christy drove. The presence of several trucks and cars showed that some of his flock had arrived.

Inside he led her to a well-used-looking lounge where eight or ten kids were busy arguing and opening cans of soda. They stopped in order to greet Christy with delighted expressions and an avalanche of questions. He held them off long enough to introduce Robbie. Although she soon lost track of the Marys and Pats and Jimmys she felt quite comfortable in the friendly atmosphere. Someone sat her in an armchair and pressed a soda into her hand and she settled down to watch.

Christy, who looked larger than life in any company, benefited even more from the contrast with his kids. If he had ever suffered from skinny awkwardness at their age, he had grown out of it and into a mature, agile grace of body and manner. Though he never appeared to be running the meeting, he listened intently and always managed to step in with the precise comment or question that would make sense out of any argument. The kids accepted his sparsely given views with a grave attention that spoke of true respect. They clearly did not regard him as an antagonist from the older generation, and he, in his turn, was careful not to bulldoze over their opinions. Robbie recalled all he had said about what he hoped to accomplish for the culture of his land, and looked at him with new respect of her own. The plan that these kids had come up with fell far short of his highest goals, but Christy supported them on every point and helped them resolve a few remaining problems. His talk about the importance of young people finding their own way had not been empty rhetoric. Robbie did not need any more reason to admire him; why couldn't he have turned out to be a hypocrite?

After two hours of lively, fruitful discussion, Christy said something that very nearly earned him Robbie's dislike. He wrapped up the work segment of the meeting and called for everyone's attention.

"Now that we're all squared away for tomorrow, we can get to the fun stuff. By sheer idiot good fortune— certainly not by any brilliant planning of my own—I've brought you a special treat tonight—a guest speaker, though I may have forgotten to warn her about it."

Robbie sat bolt upright in her chair and stared at him in horror. *Guest speaker?*

"Robbie here is not just a random American tourist," he continued, an audacious smile illuminating his face. "She's a record producer, originally from New York and now working on a project in Dublin—for Lawless Records. I know I haven't given her the chance to prepare for this, but maybe she'll be willing to answer a few questions anyway. Robbie?"

Hot-faced and self-conscious, Robbie obeyed his gesture and came up to the table at the front of the room. There was a burst of good-natured applause and encouraging comments that put her a bit more at ease.

"Well," she began nervously. "Christy's big mistake today was letting me see how competent you guys are to handle your own affairs. If I kill him after we leave here, no one will miss him, right?"

Christy cowered theatrically while her audience laughed.

"Seriously though, it sounds as if you know radio work a hell of a lot better than I do, so I won't presume to say anything about that. What else can I tell you?"

One girl spoke up, "I daresay half the people in this room would give a leg to have a real-live job in rock...oh, all right, Brandon, *two* legs...anyway, how did *you* get to be a producer and who have you produced?"

Robbie gave them a capsule version of her career, going heavy on the funny stuff and light on such trouble as Simon. In their young eyes she saw friendly interest grow to outright awe. They *knew* the bands she had worked with, and seemed to think that having Robbie in their midst was tantamount to being visited by a star.

Someone remarked fervently, "Boy, Ireland must be another world than you're used to."

"It is," Robbie agreed, timidly sneaking a glance at Christy and seeing only an artfully veiled expression on his face. "When I get back to New York I'll probably want to bring my bands over here to record. It's such a more relaxed atmosphere."

"You mean slow."

"No, not at all. For instance, at Emerald their staff is one of the most professional bunches of people I've ever worked with. Everything gets done on time—as much as it does anywhere, at least—the equipment is well maintained and they can always spare a moment to talk over a problem or jolly someone out of a bad mood. Nobody is so frazzled that they look like they've just stuck their toe in an electrical outlet."

"But don't you feel like you've dropped off the face of the earth over here? I mean, Ireland is hardly the hit capital of the universe."

Robbie paused carefully. She knew this question came from the same kind of longings she had had as a teenager—the need to be in the center of what she thought the only worthwhile activity in the world— rock. It was the fear that the truly exciting people and events would pass you by if you weren't right on top of them. She had felt that for a while, until she discovered her stronger love was for the music itself, but she remembered and understood. Mairead was an example of the same anxiety. She thought that everything worth knowing about was happening outside of Ireland.

Robbie answered ironically but truthfully, "Actually, I've come to realize that I always feel that way even in New York. Some people have a talent for setting trends or even for *following* them. I always seem to be floating along in my own world."

"But you've produced at least three songs that have gone top ten in the past half year. You *are* a trend."

Robbie made a face and they all laughed. "If I am it's been a total accident, believe me. I just keep on producing the music I like. If there's a big market for it, it sells well. If not it sells less well, but it's still there for *my* satisfaction. That seems like a pretty good guide for life actually. If I went chasing after hits, eventually I'd bomb and then I'd have to consider myself a failure. I happen to think I have impeccable taste in music—to say nothing of being fabulously talented—and I feel that, during its wiser and more lucid moments, the world will agree with me. But if it doesn't—that's *it's* loss."

"So speaks a brash Yankee!"

She countered unarguably, "Hey, I never heard it said that the *Irish* were exactly *meek* either."

"That'll be the day!" they agreed with pride in at least this one native trait.

On that high note Christy ended Robbie's public appearance. The kids organized themselves to leave, joking and jostling. Several made their way over to Robbie and extracted her promise to attend their first broadcast the next day and the party that would follow. When Christy caught her eye a thrill of intense pleasure buoyed her; the look of veiled scrutiny had given way to approval. It had taken a lot of trust to ask her to talk to his kids. He had not rehearsed her ahead of time so that she wouldn't undermine his work. She might easily have built New York into a wonderland and rock into a fairy-tale life, for all he knew. That would certainly not have helped these kids develop an appreciation for their own country. How could he trust her with this one paramount area of his life, yet not trust her with his love?

It was not the kind of question one could come out with in so many words. Robbie regretfully pushed it to the sidelines of her mind and returned with him to the car. On the short ride back to Dunquin Christy kept to light talk, so impersonal she could recall more intimate conversations with strangers on checkout lines. He seemed to suffer from spontaneous, unwilling flashes of great warmth and then subside into a grim apprehension that carved lines into his smooth brow. Did his deep-set eyes carry such an eloquent expression of suffering through some mere anatomical quirk? She should not be so quick to read misery into his face.

The sight of her own cottage was almost welcome. She also shouldn't allow herself to get too used to Christy's company like this. Going with him to the meeting had given her a misleading feeling that she *belonged* with him, when actually she had shared that tiny part of his life by accident. How *could* she fit into his master plan? She represented the world that had nearly erased Ireland. No matter how wholesome she might be personally, she was not the example he wanted to place before his kids.

He *himself* was the example—he had given up a life of easy excitement, of power and influence in an internationally glamorous field. With his very life he proved there was something of value in this land.

Adopting a bright but bland manner, Robbie hopped out of the car and threw a casual goodbye over her shoulder. "Thanks, Christy—for the rescue and for the chance to meet your kids. I'll just pull the bike off the back and..."

"Don't bother yourself—unless you want it for tomorrow, that is."

"No."

"Then I can drop it off at the inn."

"Okay. Thanks." No further reason remained to hang around his car. Robbie turned to go.

"See you at breakfast," came his unexpected promise.

"Oh! Sure." Then she did go, pondering his motives. Breakfast?

Each previous morning at Mrs. Foley's Robbie had rolled out of bed into jeans and a sweatshirt, and staggered to breakfast at the old inn. This morning she chose her least ratty pair of jeans, a good sweater, and dusted a suggestion of makeup onto her face, although she knew it would be battered off by the sea wind within five minutes of leaving the cottage. That was as close to dressing up as she dared get. Rationally, she knew that any attempt to look attractive to Christy was doomed to backfire. He did seem to find her attractive, and where had it gotten them? But her feminine instincts had risen to the top of her mind and demanded attention.

Christy sat in the parlor all by himself, reading the morning paper and absently sipping tea from Mrs. Foley's good china. Robbie stole in softly so she could have a few moments to enjoy this unguarded view of him. Vibrant life sparkled through his golden body like light through amber. Now that she knew what he felt like, tasted like, how his heart sounded when it beat close to her ear, how he smelled like wool and lime and musk, she could no longer look at him through eyes alone. Every glimpse of him saturated her anew with those sensations. She should have skipped breakfast.

Before she had quite shrugged off his effect, he looked up and the teacup paused halfway to his mouth. For a measureless fraction of a second his reactions froze as had the teacup. The fear stabbed her that he would have preferred not to see her. Then his smile appeared like the first streak of blue in a storm-heavy sky.

"Good morning—I didn't know if you had kept to your nocturnal schedule out here or not. The country folk are up with the hens."

She groaned dramatically. "I don't know about hens, but they've got plenty of roosters around here—loud ones. No, I've adjusted to the daylight hours. What's the old saying?—'When in Kerry, do as the Kerrymen do.'"

He set down his cup and hooked his strong fingers delicately around the fragile handle of the pot. "Does that include tea, or should I ask Mary to bring in some coffee for you?"

"Tea is fine." Fascinated by his little ritual of pouring the tea for her, Robbie sat down in the armchair across from him. "Is it true you make Mairead eat your cooking when she's staying with you?"

To her delight he blushed. "The girl would live on beer and chips left to herself. You have to put something good into her...."

"Is your cooking good?"

"I manage to stay somewhere between burnt and raw," he mumbled self-consciously.

"Why, Christy, aren't Irish men supposed to be able to cook?"

He grinned, having adjusted to her line of teasing. "In point of fact, we haven't come quite so far. Cooking's still the domain of good Irish girls. But—" his eyes twinkled then slid away "—as I mentioned before—no good Irish girl will ever have me...."

His revelation was interrupted by Mary's entry into the room. For three mornings Mrs. Foley had brought Robbie breakfast and chatted her ear off. Today her daughter brought the tray and, from the shy blush that stole into the girl's fair cheeks when she set a plate of eggs in front of Christy, Robbie figured out why. Mary's talk was reduced to breathless monosyllables, her movements were shy and quick as those of a bird. Once she had laid the table she dashed for the door to the kitchen but hung there a second to steal one more look at Christy. He noticed nothing.

Robbie waited until Mary had gone from earshot, then she leaned forward and remarked quietly, "There's one good Irish girl who would have you."

Christy dropped his butter knife, looking unnecessarily alarmed. "Nonsense!"

Robbie pressed on, amazed to have found a subject that disconcerted him so. "And there weren't any of those girls last night who didn't have a crush on you." She forestalled his denial by asserting mysteriously, "A woman can tell."

"Can she now? And did this particular woman happen to notice how the lads reacted to *her*?"

"What? Oh, that was just ... I mean they were just interested because I've met all these musicians they like. They're star-struck just like your sister."

"They are indeed—all of them. You can't imagine how many weeks I worked with them before they finally stopped asking for tickets to so-and-so's concert and could I get so-and-so to come out and give a guitar clinic? Once they got it through their heads that I wasn't there to spoon-feed them gossip and favors they settled down to work. But they never really got it out of their systems—it's part of being young, I suppose."

"It is?"

A great, dark weight of distress seemed to shadow him. "Don't you think so?"

"No! Oh gosh, no...I mean, I could never give it up. I'd feel like I was walking around with a hole in me. I'll find some way to stay involved in music no matter how old I get."

He stared moodily into his tea and didn't answer. Tense and perplexed, Robbie perched on the edge of her seat and suffered from the knowledge that she had hurt him. As Mairead had already suggested, whether Christy would admit it or not, he had never quite patched over the hole rock music had left in his own life. She noisily shuffled the utensils on the table, trying to break the mood. "So what are your plans today? Before the broadcast, that is."

"I'm driving into Tralee to tactfully remind a politician that he'd promised to be at the broadcast tonight. How about you?"

"I don't know. It occurs to me that I've been over here weeks and weeks and haven't bought a single gift for anyone I know. I don't even think I've sent a postcard."

His grin outshone the gloom that had momentarily eclipsed him. "Now what kind of a tourist are you?"

"Rotten."

"I'll drop you in Dingle on my way out this morning. Mary or her mother can bring you back later and you can spend an hour or two injecting your lovely Yankee dollars into the economy."

"Sounds good to me. When are you leaving?"

"As soon as I dust the crumbs off my fingers."

How he had gotten crumbs on his fingers, Robbie couldn't imagine—neither of them had eaten a thing. But she hurriedly set down her cup and ran to collect her things from the cottage so as not to hold him up.

His spirits seemed totally recovered on the road. They joked about politicians and opening-night jitters. He gave her snippets of information about the local history and geography that only a deep fondness for the area would have caused anyone to learn. Then he dropped her off in front of one of Dingle's many pastel-hued shops and headed for the mountains between there and Tralee. She caught herself smiling and humming happily as she strolled down the main street; she told herself to stop, but she was doing it again when she walked in to the first woolen shop.

"Robbie?" The caller's head emerged from behind a stack of softly colored blankets. A slender adolescent body followed and Robbie recognized Johanna, one of the kids from Christy's radio project. "That *was* you I saw roll by just now in Christy's car."

"Oh yes, he gave me a lift into town."

"Where's he off to?"

"Tralee—he's courting a politician for your broadcast tonight."

The girl's freckled face made an exaggerated grimace. "Ach, don't remind me. Declan was just in here pretending he's been a deejay for twenty years, but you just *wait* for his voice to crack on the air. Andy will never let him forget it."

"Who's Andy?"

Johanna hugged a sweater she had been folding. "He's my...uh, my..."

"Ah."

"You met him last night—the boy with the curly black hair."

"Oh yes. He's very handsome."

"And doesn't he know it, the bold fellow! He thinks he's the darling of every female from here to Dublin."

"And is he?"

"I'm afraid so!" Johanna admitted with obvious pride. "I love it when Christy comes to town—all the girls are wild for him. It's 'Christy this' and 'Christy that.' They leave Andy lying in the dust, and don't I rub it in! He needs taking down a peg or two, and I don't know where you'd find someone gorgeous enough to do it, if not Christy. You're lucky *he's* no peacock."

"*I'm* lucky? Oh, I think you've mistaken the situation...Christy and I aren't...I mean, we only know each other through his sister Mairead."

Johanna's unbelieving frown shut her up. "Well," the girl replied tartly. "Maybe they do things differently in America, but if a man looked at me the way Christy looks at you I'd go after him with a net."

Robbie felt slightly dizzy. "Bad subject, Johanna."

"No—now, Robbie darling, let me tell you the facts of life in Dingle." Assuming a solemnly maternal manner, the spindly teenager draped her arm over Robbie's shoulder. "You see, Robbie, Christy's a bit of a favorite with us around here. The Lawlesses have been coming to Dunquin for years, so we feel like they're our own, and Christy even more so because he's taken a special interest in us. And, well...we're all starting to wonder when he's going to settle down, have a few kids of his own—we don't want him to go to waste, you see."

Robbie was caught between anxiety and laughter. Johanna sounded like some matriarch concerned over her wayward offspring. Still, Robbie didn't like several of the directions in which this monologue might go. She kept her mouth closed and her expression equally so.

Johanna studied her through her lashes and went on without encouragement. "I don't want to give you the impression that we're a bunch of clucking busybodies—even if we are—but he's never been interested in anyone here and he's never brought anyone out with him from Dublin before...."

"Johanna! He didn't bring *me* here from Dublin—it was *coincidence*."

The girl nodded briskly, acknowledging and dismissing Robbie's claim at the same time. "However it happened, the fact is...the fact is..." Suddenly she seemed to have lost her nerve.

Robbie wondered if it was the warning glower she had focused on the girl.

Johanna straightened and finished with a bright blush, "The fact is, I'm running over at the mouth, aren't I? You don't need my advice.... Look, why don't you tell me what you're in the market for and I'll point you to the right shelves?"

It took Robbie a second or two to switch gears. What she was in the market for? Oh, of course—*sweaters*!

Chapter Eight

Whether it was out of respect for the kids' endeavor, because of the chance of a parliamentary representative being present or because she knew she would have Christy's eyes upon her all evening, Robbie dressed with what she would have once considered obsessive care. For the entire six weeks in Ireland she had lugged around two party dresses—a strange black thing that Simon had picked out, and an ivory-colored silk with boxy shoulders and a straight, elegant silhouette. In a typical fit of extravagance, Simon had brought her back from Japan an opera-length strand of pearls and matching earrings. The warm, creamy tones glowed against her Mediterranean skin and made her eyes sparkle with greens and browns. Though she could think of nothing special to do with her hair, having cared little about her looks for most of her life, she brushed it until it shimmered as lustrously as the silk dress and she decided she'd pass. At least she would contrast with her usual "thrown-together" look.

Christy picked her up in the little red car, as usual, but he seemed distracted as he drove—the planning and dreaming in private was over, tonight his kids were laying themselves on the line. Tonight they had to stand or fall in the eyes of the world—at least a small part of the world.

Christy looked wonderful in his fawn-brown suit. With a deft sense of color, he had complemented it with a slate-blue shirt and coppery tie. His hair shone with every kind of gold, his deep-set eyes reflected the late afternoon sun.

"Did you get the political guy to come tonight?" Robbie asked, thinking that if it had been a woman, Christy would have had no problem.

"I did indeed—Deputy Timothy Stone. I had to point out to him that this show appealed to kids who would be of voting age in a very few years."

"Well, of course. What did you expect from a professional politician?"

Christy's mobile eyebrows swung into an expression of chagrin. "I tend to forget that not everybody automatically understands how important these kids are. The politicians have to be educated a good deal more than *they* do."

"I happened upon Johanna Morrissey in Dingle today. We had a chat."

He seemed pleased to have his mind taken off the coming broadcast. "Did you now? What about?"

"Oh," Robbie began vaguely—how much could she tell him? "Just things...Has anybody considered cable TV shows for these kids? Rock video is so popular in the U.S.'' She hoped he wouldn't notice how quickly she had abandoned the subject she had just brought up.

"We've got no cable capability so far—but videos are popular here, too—it's only a matter of time, I expect."

"Will you be branching out into TV?"

"You're such an ambitious little thing!" he observed in amusement. "But yes, I've been told I get a gleam in my eye when someone mentions television. Do I?''

She pretended to study him scrupulously, although she could hardly analyze a face that caused her such emotional disorder. "Hmm—now that you mention it, I do see a definite manic glint. You probably *scared* Deputy Stone into coming."

"Well, if it works, I'll use it."

The studio buzzed with excitement. No matter how prepared the kids might be for their professional duties, they were still young. Christy made one circuit through the studio, greeting and calming everyone, and then he confined himself to the lounge where many friends, relatives and well-wishers were gathered. A couple of kids ran in to consult him or beg for his last-minute help, but he replied calmly and threw them back on their own resources. Robbie approved; she handled young bands the same way. There came a time when they had to develop confidence in *themselves*.

The politician showed up at the last minute. Christy strode forward to shake his hand and settle him in a strategic chair. Tension mounted. Robbie felt herself grow alternately flushed and chilled, as though she had an immense personal stake in this project. The worst moments came as the adult deejay of the preceding show closed his program of sports news. Then the theme music switched. The professional in Robbie noted the nice fresh feel of the music the kids had chosen and wondered if it was the work of one of their local bands.

The woman in Robbie stole a glance at Christy. He stood with casual grace by the politician's chair. The hand that reposed in one trouser pocket flared back his jacket and revealed his trim hips. In contrast, Timothy Stone, who couldn't have had many years on Christy, looked pudgy and sallow. Robbie cautioned herself not to be so critical. Her own world had its share of unhealthy specimens. Even Simon, vain as he was, had the start of a spare tire at his waist.

The first words of the broadcast crowded these idle observations out of Robbie's head. Declan, the boy who had been chosen as deejay, launched boldly into the show and commanded every scrap of her attention. After a few minutes his obvious control of the situation dissolved the tension in the room. His voice did not crack. The careful silence of the well-wishers was broken by delighted, half-giddy comments. Timothy Stone quipped that he'd like to take public-speaking lessons from the young fellow. A few of the more intrepid parents danced when the music came on. Even Christy's cheeks blossomed with the telltale pink of pleasure. Robbie thought she had never seen him look so handsome. He had poured so much of his beautiful soul into this project and happiness fairly burst from him.

The ninety-minute broadcast seemed to race by. Suddenly Declan had plugged in the closing theme, and a few seconds later his sunny face appeared at the door of the lounge. All the kids who had been at their work stations monitoring the show streamed in with joy and congratulations. It seemed as if the party would get into full swing there in the lounge but, inspired by their success as broadcasters, the kids quickly recovered their senses and sent everyone on their way to the parish hall.

Out of the corner of her eye, Robbie watched Christy. He had, of course, taken Stone as his personal responsibility. She wondered if she should get a lift from Johanna so that he could chauffeur the deputy, but before she had threaded her way through the crowded halls to the parking lot, Christy beckoned for her to meet him outside.

"Well, you look smug," she observed when they met at the car. Robbie herself felt swollen with pride on his behalf. If this broadcast represented only the tiniest step in his plan, it was still a wonderful achievement for the group of young people he had guided.

"They did well, didn't they?" he asked with touching eagerness.

"They did indeed. If they run the party as well as they ran the show, they can open up a professional catering business."

The party was a much less formal affair and lacked the palest ghost of seriousness. Robbie had never seen a group of people so giddy; it took her half an hour to notice that there wasn't an alcoholic beverage in sight, just a band playing Irish music with almost drunken exuberance. The excitement bubbled irrepressibly into dancing—rock, disco, ballroom, Irish. Robbie muddled her way through a crash course in the traditional group dances that every member of the congregation knew, from the eldest granny on down to the toddlers. All the dances she had ever been to had involved dates and lack of dates and thus could never be enjoyed for the sheer thrill of music and movement. She ducked out

of the patterns to fan herself again and again, only to
be snagged for yet another whirl.

Every once in a while she found herself swept across
the floor in Christy's strong arms. She had never seen
him so buoyant, so free of care. He had tossed his jacket
carelessly over a chair, and his coppery tie whipped
across his shoulders as he moved. He threw himself into
dancing with all his irresistible vitality. By the end of the
evening Robbie felt like a drenched rag and he still
bloomed.

The party broke up long before any New York party
would have. Robbie realized it was a school night. The
politician had long ago gone off to a pub with a local
magistrate to prepare himself for his drive back to Tralee. Once more Christy met Robbie in the parking lot.

Though the flaming sunset betokened clouds somewhere out at sea, the sky directly above was clear, and
the moon lit the fern-covered hills like a cool, silvery
sun. A vigorous wind had started. The sound of waves
and shivering bracken made Robbie stand still next to
the car. She felt a wordless harmony between this tough
invigorating landscape and the music that poured from
bands like the one that had played at the party. Here in
Kerry, with no concrete avenues to block it and no ve-
neer of sophistication to dull it, the feeling of life and
possibility swept free, as fierce and brash as this night
wind.

As she let it fill her heart and her lungs, she became
aware of Christy's intense gaze. She shivered abruptly.

"What's the matter?" came his soft question.

"Nothing. Nothing at all. It's just..." She had no
words for the contentment that had held her for one
clear, silvery moment. She finished inadequately, "It's
just so beautiful here."

He nodded, not a shallow, social nod, but one that communicated deep understanding. She saw the wind carve channels in his hair and poke playfully under the folds of his jacket. Even in his fine clothes he seemed a natural extension of the elements. Unwilling to let her thoughts go further, Robbie ducked into the car. After a beat he followed, casting her a surprisingly tentative smile. He turned the key in the ignition and shifted smoothly into gear.

This time the sight of her own cottage glowing white in the distance was unwelcome. She had allowed herself to get too familiar with Christy's company again. To leave him for the empty rooms inside would be too hard; better to take a short walk and try to dispel her melancholy.

"Will you drop me at the beach?" she asked, her voice awkward in the silence. "I want to take a short walk while there's such a nice moon."

"Surely."

The beach lay barely a third of a mile from the cottage but the trip provided a few more moments of Christy's company. She sighed as the car's high beams swept the little notch of sand at the end of the road. It stopped and Christy turned the headlights off.

"Here we are. You're not going to clamber around on the rocks, are you?"

"No, I'll stick to the sand."

"In those shoes?" He raised an eyebrow at her high heels.

"Oops. I guess I'll take them off. What's a pair of stockings anyway?"

"Or frozen feet."

"Exactly." She paused, wondering how to thank him without baring the loneliness in her heart. "It was very special tonight. It meant a lot to me to see what you've been doing; I understand it better now.''

''I thought you would.''

In the darkness she could not read his expression, though his voice was deep and warm. She decided she'd better get out of the car. ''Well, good night then.'' She set off across the sand before he could catch a hint of her desolation.

The roughness of the wind and spray from the open Atlantic pleased her and gave her something to think about rather than the enigmatic man she had just left. Holding her shoes, she picked her way through the cold tidal pools that shone like mirrors under the moon.

With half an ear she waited for the sound of the car driving away; it never came. She stole a look over her shoulder and saw its dim outline in the moonlight. She turned away hunched into the wind.

The car door slammed. She stood at the edge of the sea, immobile but for her shivering, afraid to even think the thoughts that had surged up at that one sound. It took all her willpower not to turn around and check to see if he was really walking across the sand, drawing nearer and nearer. For all the evidence her ears gave her he might have stepped out of the car and vanished off the face of the earth. Then she felt, or imagined that she felt, a faint flare of heat against her back. He said nothing but she knew he was close enough to touch, close enough that, if she swayed back ever so slightly, she could tip her head onto the powerful swell of his chest. As automatically as breathing, her body followed her thought. His arms swept around her and tightened into a warm, sweet cocoon of strength. He buried his roughened cheek into the curve where her neck flowed into her shoulder, and the sound that rose from his chest was so raw only her heart could understand it.

Arms locked over the tops of his, knowing that she held him up as much as he held her, Robbie let the moment spin out into an infinite dream. She didn't know when it would end, or what she would learn from his eyes when he faced her again, but his body spoke to her right then and told her of his love.

When he finally turned her in his arms, the fire in his burnt-black eyes acknowledged the message that had passed between them. But it had brought him no peace. If *she* had found herself confused, he was clearly torn by some private struggle. She knew she could demand nothing, no explanation of the hell he had put her through, no clarification of his worry, no promises for the future . . . he would not know what to tell her.

She let him release her and take her hand in his own time. Side by side they left the beach, passed his car without a glance and walked up the empty road to her cottage. As they mounted the steps of the porch the world slowed to a wordless pantomime; he took the keys from her hand, unlocked the door and pushed it open. He slid his strong, tender fingers through her tangled hair and delicately held her face still while he searched it for something, some clue or sign. Then, eyes closed to a fringe of sooty lash, he bent close and touched her with a kisslike breath. She waited, but there was no more. He pulled himself determinedly away and backed down to the first step. Stifling a sob, Robbie forced herself into the cottage and closed the door between them.

She stood far enough from the window for the darkness within to swallow her. Through the glass she watched Christy walk to his car. Then she resolutely drew the curtains. Whatever troubled him so bitterly, she had the feeling that he had to wrestle it to some kind of a conclusion without her.

Robbie's determination to leave Christy alone lasted halfway through the night and no longer. She had bundled herself in a woolly afghan and sat by the cold fireplace, staring at a book. Unfortunately, it was a very sexy book, but not otherwise interesting. Her eyes drifted again and again to the window, watching as the lights turned on and off at Christy's cottage—first in the kitchen, then in the bedroom and finally in the living room. These last never went dark. He seemed to have been stricken with the same insomnia that held her.

She made coffee, she ironed a couple of shirts, she flipped through the magazines Mrs. Foley had brought over. The light next door stayed on; Robbie stayed awake. She had intended to give Christy every chance to decide how he felt about her and call her to him in his own time...or not. But finally she could stand herself no longer. She shook off the unnatural passivity that had afflicted her; since when had she *waited* for things to happen? She would still be hanging around street corners if she hadn't talked her way into the gofer job at Soho Sound. She'd still be Simon's assistant if she hadn't jumped on those independent projects. Then again, if she hadn't snapped up this Fire Hazard project she'd still be back in New York blissfully ignorant of the existence of Christy O'Laighleis.

That line of thought would drive her crazy, as would twiddling her thumbs and sweating while not two hundred feet away, Christy O'Laighleis decided their fate.

Obeying a sudden sense of urgency, Robbie threw the afghan over her head and stepped out into the night. It was finally raining in Ireland. She toyed with the idea that the break in the weather was symbolic of her decision to let her emotions guide her, but it didn't quite fit—the rain should have been a drenching downpour. It ought to be the tumultuous, raging storm of gothic novels, which drove the heroine into the arms of her hero and provided a suitably violent background for their passion. Instead it was an annoying drizzle.

By the time she had squished her way across the soggy grass to Christy's her hair had frizzed up into little corkscrews and she felt clammy all over, not great preparation to meet a lover. She rapped on the door and waited. She was about to call his name when it swung open. Christy glared at her, so ominous in the shadow that Robbie hung back. He looked different, apart from the glower, which to be honest, she had seen before. He looked *untidy*. For once his tight, mobile body looked as if it might not belong to his brain—he slouched, his reflexes were strangely slow, even his breathing seemed labored. Gone was the usual crisp suit and spotless sweater; in the dank, cold air he stood there in a white T-shirt and slacks. A suspicious flush spread through his bare arms and neck.

Robbie stared at him in surprise, then looked beyond into the cottage. A bright fire gave deceptive cheeriness to the dark room. She saw no sign of activity—no work papers, no opened books, no TV, no music, just a half-empty bottle of whiskey on the coffee table, and a glass beside it.

He noticed the direction of her gaze and said deliberately, "Join me?"

"In getting drunk?"

"Footless," he replied. "On a tear, away with the Bann, stocious—you may as well learn some native slang while you're on holiday. And speaking of which, what bloody business of yours is it how *I* spend my free time?"

Stunned by such hostility, Robbie gaped. Then she recovered, reminding herself that she was there to influence his decision in a *favorable* direction. "You're drunk and I'm wet. May I come in?"

He blinked inscrutable eyes, then stepped back and extravagantly waved her inside.

Though the outer reaches of the room were chilly, the fire created a cozy circle of warmth. She wandered at its edge, dropping her damp afghan over a chair and feeling Christy's scrutiny like a cold draft.

"Why are you here, girl?" he asked in a low, burred voice. Whiskey had brought out the tooth of his brogue.

Robbie felt speared upon this crucial moment. She knew it must be fairly obvious to him why she had come, but she couldn't flail around anymore in a sea of half-understood words and gestures and imaginings, she had to say it aloud.

She clasped her hands together in a fretful knot and let her eyes skitter randomly over the contents of the room, over everything but Christy. Her voice emerged weaker and more anxious than she had hoped. "I guess we've already established that I'm not too... uh... experienced with men... That is..."

Disconcertingly he left the pool of shadow in which he had stood after closing the door, and began to prowl across the floor, passing slowly behind her, so close the hair rose on the back of her neck.

"Have you come to me for advice, perhaps?"

"Don't joke, Christy, please. This is hard for me."

"I know," he whispered wretchedly.

"I'm *confused*. I don't know what to expect from you. One minute you treat me as if you...might care for me and the next..."

"The next minute I'm a beast, a surly, miserable beast."

This was a little more severe than what Robbie would have said, but Christy seemed to think it barely sufficient. He raked his hand roughly through his hair, separating it into dark-gold segments that fell ungovernably across his face. He walked around to the front of the couch and threw himself down within reach of the whiskey. He seemed disinclined to talk.

Robbie eased herself onto the cushions at the open end of the couch. She had no idea how to proceed; inspiration stubbornly refused to rescue her. She asked lamely, "Christy, tell me what's going on."

"What do you *think* is going on?"

She couldn't take any more, her answer came out in a plaintive wail. "I think I'm in love with you."

His cold disinterest vanished, to be replaced by a look of acute pain. "Don't think that, darling. Don't think that *at all*." He rubbed his face fretfully in his hands, swearing a torrent of inarticulate curses. When he took his hands away his face burned with an earnest fire. "How I wish you *weren't* so bloody innocent! This isn't some fairy-tale land, somehow free of the rules that apply to New York or wherever else you consider real life. Quaint Eireann, the Emerald isle, land of lachrymose poets weeping in their beer..."

Too taken aback to reply, she stared wide-eyed as he took a deep, ragged breath and leaned in for a further attack.

"Is that it? Do you think we need only fall into bed with each other tonight and all the problems that divide us will disappear?"

Unknown to her, tears streamed unchecked down her face.

Christy's voice filled with a sorrowful tenderness. "I wish I had a druid's magic in these hands, my love. I'd wipe away all our differences just like this..." He reached out one reluctant hand and traced his fingertips through the wetness on her cheeks. She grabbed his hand compulsively and held it away, unable to bear the torment of his touch. He should have hit her or yelled or thrown her out into the rain.

Instead, entirely contrary to his words, he pressed her back into the cushions and enveloped her in the heat and strength of passion. Though her mind was more bewildered than ever, her body knew exactly what to do. Her hands swept up his waist, over the powerful muscles that sheathed his ribs; she clutched his shoulders with every ounce of strength she possessed. Her legs tangled with his and liquefied in the fire he had ignited inside her. His mouth, bearing down upon hers, brought more pain than pleasure, but did not satisfy her need to become even more a part of him. Even when his lips left hers and traveled searchingly down her throat into the open neck of her shirt, and burned kisses onto the soft flesh of her breast, she struggled to bring him closer. Druid's magic indeed. Every glowing inch of his skin changed the substance of her world to fire, radiant and all-consuming. What more could magic do than melt and recast life?

Then a shudder ran through him and she felt a change in his embrace. He no longer seemed to seek her but to be retreating into himself. *Why did he always pull away?*

She had made no case of the problems between them. Distraught because she could think of no remedy, she watched him bury his face between her breasts and gasp. Stroking his hair, she pleaded, "What differences are stronger than this, Christy?"

"Don't you see it?" he whispered harshly. He dragged his face up and looked into her eyes with his soul laid bare. "Don't you know what's about to happen to you? Your album with Two Time just went platinum, so did two of the singles off it. Mairead tells me that when you're done with her record you're off to France to do a soundtrack album for some fifty-million-dollar Hollywood epic. A fellow I know at Lawless says that one of the big British labels has been calling all this past week trying to locate you but Shaw won't tell them where you are—he intends to sign you to an exclusive contract with Lawless when you get back."

Robbie's head reeled. "What label? No, no, never mind. I still don't see what bothers you...."

With a great effort, Christy hauled the two of them upright and sat cupping both her hands in his. "The fact is, Robbie Calderón is one very hot young rock producer."

"So what?"

"So, Ireland is a little backwater. It's a big enough place for you now while you're doing Fire Hazard's album, and while...while you feel something for me." He placed his finger over her lips to stop her protest. "But the world is out there waiting for you. You'll leave and give Ireland hardly a backward glance. Shh...don't argue with me now. I *know* what your life is going to be like. I've seen it before, remember? You're on the verge of major success. It doesn't happen to many people and I'd never try to take it from you."

"But..."

He shook his head at her.

To herself she contradicted. But I don't want major success, I want *you*. She did't say it. Desperate as she was, she knew it would sound like fatuous, love-besotted drivel, and he'd never take her seriously. Instead she said, "You don't give me much credit, do you? You think I'll get so full of my own importance that I'll never come back to Ireland."

"No, that's not it at all...but I don't want to have you just on weekends, or every other month when you can sneak me a visit in between jobs. I want to be your life—or at least to share it all with you. And I won't follow you from recording studio to recording studio—not because of any stupid, male pride, but because I just can't be a part of that rock life anymore. I've had it and I don't want it anymore."

"That doesn't leave us with much, does it?" she asked weakly. He did not bother to answer. She gently extricated her hands from his; there wasn't much point in hanging on to each other if, in his mind, he had already let her go. She dragged herself off the couch, surprised that her legs had any strength. "I won't see you in Dublin then, will I?"

He mouthed a silent "no." She nodded and let her numbed feet carry her out into the night.

Chapter Nine

When Robbie awoke the next morning to an appropriately dingy mist, the little red car was gone. She had expected as much. Her meeting with Christy here in storm-dashed Kerry had been an accident for everyone except Mairead, the debacle that followed a hopeless farce. To see him anymore would be fruitless and painful, why should he stick around?

For lack of anything better to do she went out for a walk. She heard her name called from the inn and saw Mary launch herself out into the yard at a brisk trot.

"Robbie! Robbie! You have a telephone call from Dublin!"

Robbie never ran for the telephone—whom in Dublin could she want to hear from anyway? But Mary seemed unnerved by the fact that this was long distance and so Robbie broke her habit and sprinted to the inn.

"Hello?" she panted into the heavy black phone in the hallway.

"Robbie!" Michael Shaw's voice. "My God, you're out and about at an ungodly hour."

"So are you, Michael. What's up?" She tried to inject a little enthusiasm into her voice and knew she had failed.

"Oh, I crawl out to the newsagents to get the trades one morning a week—one of the bad habits you Americans got me into. I just wanted to tell you, in case you're rusticating too much out there, that an old friend of yours has been burning up the phone lines from London to my office trying to get in touch with you."

Robbie suddenly had a sinking feeling. "Who?"

"Simon Beyer...Robbie, are you there?"

"Yeah, but evidently even *here* is not far enough out to avoid hearing his name again."

"That fond of him, are you? He acted as if you two were inseparable."

"History."

"I guess it's a good thing I didn't tell him where you were."

"Yeah, except he'd never come out here to see me. If he's not in a five-star hotel with closed circuit TV and an after-hours club he goes into withdrawal. Did he say there was any special reason he wanted me, or was it just a general annoyance call?"

"A little of both, I think. I've got his number in London if..."

"Burn it."

"When are you coming back? Mairead was in here the other day and I asked if she had heard from you. She told me to mind my own business. I thought she was a bit snippy about it, too. But when are you coming back?"

Here was a question. Did it serve any further purpose to stay in Kerry? One way or another the album had been cleared from her mind; she might as well go back now. The quicker she got the mix-down done, the quicker she could leave Ireland and start clearing Christy from her mind as well. The thought depressed her.

"I guess I'll be back within the next couple of days. What's today? Friday? Would you give Donal Sheehy a call and ask him if we can start Monday morning?"

"Sure thing. You sound tired, Robbie."

"Too much fresh air."

She had meant that as a quip, but when she got off the train at Heuston Station she noticed the weight of ash in the Dublin air—air she had once thought incredibly pure compared to that in New York. She'd probably suffocate when she got back to the States.

Dozens of messages awaited her at her flat: greetings from friends, a few business questions from her lawyer and accountant, a pile of tapes from musicians who wanted her attention and had somehow tracked her down. Robbie accepted a tray of tea from Mrs. Hall and sat down in the sun parlor to look them over. The sudden crunch of minutiae suited her, it kept her busy when she might very well have moped. Michael had left a mysterious message that he had something to talk over with her at her leisure. This must be the exclusive contract that Christy had mentioned. An exclusive contract... The temptation to accept it was strong—the psychological and financial backing of a good company could sometimes enable a producer to take a few risks on exciting talents.

Robbie had enjoyed her association with Lawless, and she adored Emerald Studios; she suspected there were more undiscovered bands of Fire Hazard's high caliber in Ireland, and she could get a lot of satisfaction from developing them. The only problem, an insurmountable one, was that staying in Ireland meant staying within risk of Christy. She didn't even feel comfortable with the idea of seeing Simon again; the prospect of running into Christy here, there and everywhere terrified her.

Politeness and obstinate curiosity made her agree to dinner with Michael anyway. He took her to a particularly elegant restaurant, necessitating the quick drycleaning of the ivory silk dress. She met him there, knowing the choice of location was part of his sales pitch. Over very expensive white wine and paté she let him sneak up on the topic of contract.

"Did you like Kerry?"

"Oh yes." She returned what she suspected must be a fairly standard rave about the people, the landscape, etc.

"We've got mile after mile of it here in Ireland. And all so close to Dublin. Really, you can leave the studio and be settled in front of a peat fire listening to the roar of the sea in half an hour. None of the great rush-hour treks you New Yorkers endure. Robbie agreed tentatively. The thought had occurred to her more than once.

He seemed to take a deep breath. "I want you to think about staying in Ireland, Robbie."

She held her breath.

"You probably think I'm mad, trying to lure you away from the center of the music world. But I believe that you're not the kind of producer who likes to rest on her laurels. We're developing something here that has the potential to be very strong, very exciting. At Lawless we don't have as many preconceived corporate policies as the major labels elsewhere, we don't even have a big reputation to protect—or to fall back on. We're a *frontier* is what I'm trying to say to you." He paused to refill her wineglass and try to catch her eye, but she kept her gaze trained uncomfortably on the centerpiece. "You're a pioneer, Robbie. You like to carve out a wilderness, I think. Well, we've got a wilderness here all right, and we can offer you practically free rein to conquer it."

"Are you talking about a contract?"

He looked flustered. "Yes—did I forget to mention that? A minor detail..."

She tried to control the sudden thudding of her heart. "Then let me remind you of another one—I haven't finished mixing this *one* album yet. What if I bungle it? Surely your management isn't talking about signing me until they have at least heard the mix-down, and they'll probably want to wait to see how the album sells."

"Well...I might be speaking of this a wee bit prematurely, but uprooting yourself is a big step, I wanted you to be thinking about it before you had to decide."

"That's very considerate of you, Michael."

"No, just prudent. Actually, Robbie, I know you're thinking about doing that film soundtrack and I was afraid that once you slipped away you'd be gone for good."

She noticed he made no mention of any advances by a British label; undoubtedly she would discover the details in time but she had no energy to pursue it right them.

Michael looked at her brightly. "Do you have any feelings one way or the other, Robbie?"

Did she! None of them could be offered to Michael, no matter how much of a friend he had become. Her heart screamed for her to accept his offer, to dump the New York apartment into the East River and settle permanently on Northumberland Road—any part of it. That was not, however, what her rational mind told her. She shrugged. "I guess I'm going back to New York."

"You guess? Why? Can't we offer you enough interesting work?"

"No, the work sounds fine. It's just . . . I guess I just belong in New York."

"You don't sound sure. If you don't mind my saying so, Robbie, you *don't* seem like you belong in New York—at least not the New York I see when I go over there. When I met you at that party for that band . . . what was its name?"

"Vice."

"Right, Vice—you seemed like you couldn't wait to get away from those people."

"Well, some are worse than others. . . . Not everyone is like that."

"No, just the trendies. So you'll just have to stop making hits and attracting the trendy set. Or you'll have to move to Ireland."

"Hey, you're not so untouched over here, you know. There's a bit of a trendy scene over here, too—amid the gorgeous, fairy-tale scenery."

"Yes, but we're not ruined *yet*. You like working at Emerald, I think. . . ."

"Low blow! Yes, I like working there very much. They're my kind of people."

"So . . ."

"So, I'm taking them all back to New York *with* me. Can we drop the subject for now, Michael? I'm very flattered by your confidence in me, but I'm just not ready to think about it seriously."

"All right, but I've taken note that you said let's drop it *for now*. Well, what will you have for dinner?"

Monday morning Robbie dragged herself down to Emerald Studios. The whole point of a break between recording and mix-down was to recharge the mental batteries but Robbie felt like a car whose headlights had been left on overnight. Ugh, she groaned, bad analogy.

Then, entirely against her expectations, she walked into the control room, saw Donal's grimly serious face as he wrapped tape onto a spool, and felt a huge surge of optimistic energy. She *did* like her work. She had always been able to count on the studio as a refuge from the garbage that gummed up her life—not that Christy was garbage, but he *had* gummed up her life. At least for a few hours of the day she wouldn't be preyed upon by memories of his fine eyes, his gentle, tantalizing touch, his warm smell, his musical voice. . . .

In the studio she was okay. She and Donal ran through the tapes of the first song, their best chance for a hit, and she felt chills of delight. They worked quickly, aiming for a propulsive undercurrent and sparkling details. Robbie chose the tracks of each instrument based on their energy and magic, not their technical perfection.

On the first day she and Donal managed a final mix in a suspiciously short few hours. When she gave the song another listen the next day, it still sounded good. She called the band.

"Hey, I just heard this great song by a band that sounds a lot like you—want to come listen?"

In record time the whole bunch bounced into the control room. Having been allowed in it so seldom, they looked sheepish and uncomfortable. Mairead gave Robbie a sharp look, but quickly got caught up in the purpose of the visit. Robbie propped her feet on the console and signaled for Donal's assistant to run the tape.

She knew they would be pleased, but she wanted to cement their confidence in her before she went on with the rest of the album. They *were* pleased; they gloated for nearly twenty minutes, then, as was inevitable, they started to pick apart their performances and get anxious. Robbie cheerfully but firmly threw them out of the studio. "Out! Out! Go to a pub, go practice giving autographs or something. I'll call you with progress reports and I think Michael will want you for some promo stuff."

Micky agreed. "Yeah, we're supposed to go out to Athlone to have our photos taken for the cover—there's a great castle ruin nearby."

Robbie frowned. "Correct me if I'm wrong, but hasn't there *been* a castle on an album cover recently? An album by a very good, very *major* Irish band?

Eamonn grinned with his usual irreverence. "Sure—same castle, too—but we're doing a *parody* of it. They have a good sense of humor...I hope."

Then they bounded out. All but Mairead. She hung back by the door looking grave until Robbie went over to her.

"Seems like you were gone longer than two weeks, Robbie."

"Well, actually it was a little less."

"And we haven't had a chance to do any-thing...fun...you know? Girl talk, whatever."

Robbie imagined that the "girl talk" Mairead had in mind wouldn't be fun for at least one of them. She mumbled vaguely.

Mairead persisted, "Why don't you come by for a sandwich sometime?"

"Up to Howth?"

"No, I'm at Christy's house these days."

Robbie carefully said nothing, but such a wave of longing swept her that she imagined she had turned green.

Mairead's gaze narrowed almost imperceptibly. "He's in Germany for two weeks buying radio equipment for a little station that's starting up near Sligo." She finished plaintively, "I get lonely all by myself."

"Sure you do... Oh, all right, I'll drop by. Tomorrow?"

The girl brightened. "Great! Fried egg sandwiches? Ham?"

"*Nothing* fried. Do you have anything low cholesterol?"

The talk couldn't have been put off forever, not if Robbie expected to maintain any kind of good relationship with Mairead. Robbie whacked the lion-headed door knocker, thinking poignantly of how much she had come to like the girl, as more than a client, as more than even a protégée. Leaving Ireland would include leaving this other dear friend. But her brother had made it inevitable.

Mairead opened the door, swamped in the now familiar yellow Trinity College sweatshirt. Robbie smiled with what she hoped came off as lightheartedness and stepped inside. The house was a shock. She had seen Christy in it only one time, and that experience had swamped her with conflicting impressions, but now that she knew him, the house was unmistakably his. He was a passionate man striving toward idealistic goals, but he was smart enough to know they could only be achieved through the proper blend of inspiration and slow, patient work. The careful harmonies of shape and line in his house, the subtle use of texture, color and style all reflected his intense desire for that balance in his life. He had to struggle for the sort of tranquillity this house represented.

Feeling clumsy and disruptive, Robbie followed Mairead into the living room. For once the ebullient blonde seemed at a loss. She flitted about like a bird in a tree; she fussed over the cucumber sandwiches until Robbie was tempted to slap her hands; she babbled about trivia—even worse trivia than usual. Robbie had come into the house calm in the sullen sort of apathy that descended upon her when not in the studio, but after a few minutes of Mairead's fidgeting, her own nerves were jangled.

"Mairead, stop fussing with everything and sit down."

Eyes round as marbles at Robbie's peremptory tone, she fell into a chair and waited without saying a word. Robbie wished her own emotions would obey as readily as had Mairead. Even though she had taken charge of the situation, inside she felt anxiety creeping through her like a guerrilla army.

"Now look, Mairead, this beating around the bush is making me crazy! You want to ask what happened between me and your brother in Kerry, don't you?"

"Arp," Mairead responded awkwardly.

"Hey, it's okay. I realize you meant well."

Mairead stared intently at her knees. "Christy wasn't quite so understanding."

Robbie's heart thundered. She didn't like to think what Christy's reaction must have been.

"I guess I sort of set you up," the girl admitted miserably.

"Sort of?"

"Well, it was just that I thought you and he seemed to... See, he's never let himself take a woman seriously before and...well, I thought maybe if you had some time alone, maybe..." She looked up, her round face white with misery. "I only meant well."

"I know you did. But...some things either happen by themselves or they don't happen at all."

"I thought it was happening."

Robbie was lost for a reply. "It" had been happening. Mairead had not imagined the attraction between her brother and her friend, she had just mistakenly assumed that it might progress like a relationship between normal people—people who weren't committed to careers that butted heads like obstinate rams.

Robbie realized she had left Mairead's protest hanging fire. Gently, she replied, "I'm sorry, Mairead. Some things just don't work out."

Mairead's expression knotted into a scowl, her fingernails scraped the slick cotton of the chair arms. "That *beast*, he ruined it, didn't he?"

"Mairead..."

"I knew he would. He's determined to hang about with these females who have the emotional and intellectual depth of a house plant. I knew if he ever found someone good enough he'd chicken out."

Was that what he had done? Robbie considered it for a moment. Had he let her career become an obstacle, even unconsciously, so he wouldn't have to take her seriously? No, confused as she was, she knew *that* wasn't the case. He *had* taken her seriously. Mairead claimed he avoided love so he would not be hurt, but he *had* loved her, she was sure of it, and he *had* been hurt.

"Tell me, Mairead, what do you think Christy needs in a woman?"

"Huh? Well, um..." She had obviously never verbalized this before, though doubtless she had an abundant supply of opinions. "I always figured it would have to be someone like him—serious and committed to something. And I figured it wouldn't hurt if she was involved in rock. No matter how many speeches he makes, he's never lost his love for it. He won't be happy until he can work it back into his life somehow.... Was I horribly wrong?"

"Not on *every* count. 'Serious and committed' still sound good, but it has to be to something he believes in—like the future of Irish music. He may never lose his gut attraction to rock, but he won't let it get in his way, either. He's very determined."

Mairead looked up meekly. "Is that what screwed you two up? Rock getting in the way?"

"Well, let's just say that we were doomed from the start."

Mairead remained in contemplative silence. Robbie felt she had made some impression on the girl, perhaps enough to convince her that this thing with Christy—its failure—was not the result of her brother's obtuseness, or whatever a critical sister might be inclined to call it. Mairead's question, asked from the gloom of the corner in which she sat, took Robbie unaware. "What is it *you* need?"

"Me?" Robbie's nerves twinged again. "I need my career. Rock is all I've ever wanted or been able to rely on as far back as I can remember."

The singer emitted a heartfelt sigh. "I'd be the last person to argue with that."

In the following somber silence, they heard the rattle of a key in the front door lock. Mairead jumped. "Oh, damn!"

Alarmed, Robbie demanded, "Are you expecting someone?"

"No...well, that is...I sort of lied—Christy isn't leaving for Germany for a while yet, you see..."

Robbie sank faintheartedly into the couch cushions. "Oh, Mairead, you didn't think to throw us together again, did you?"

"I'm sorry! Oh, Robbie, I *am* sorry!" She jumped up, her voice a shrill whisper. "Look, just sit tight. He usually goes right upstairs to change and it's dark in here. He doesn't even have to know you're here...." She launched herself from the chair in order to intercept Christy before he had the chance to venture into the living room.

Sitting frozen in shadow while Christy walked into his own house fifteen feet away from her was one of the hardest things Robbie had ever had to do. Then she realized that everything she had done with respect to him had been hard, save only falling into his arms. She saw him step into the well-lit entry, his usual sun-drenched vitality dimmed by exhaustion and perhaps, unless she were imagining it, a touch of melancholy. The overhead light still sparked a hundred shades of gold from his hair, but his eyes looked bleak and strain pulled down the corners of his lovely mouth. His broad shoulders slumped forward; his stride was slow. And still he was the most beautiful man she had ever seen. She wrung the ends of her denim jacket into a tight wad.

"How'd it go with the cabinet minister?" Mairead asked animatedly, stepping so as to lead Christy's attention away from the living room doorway"

"It went well," he replied with a notable lack of enthusiasm. "I think he might break free a few thousand pounds for broadcasting scholarships if I can get the P.M.'s blessing."

"That's great, Christy. Lord, you must be bushed, all day and all evening with that dreary bore. I suppose you'll want to run a bath and change or something."

Don't be so overeager! Robbie prayed silently.

A wan smile flickered across Christy's face. "Are you trying to get rid of me, Mairead? Have you a guest perhaps?"

"Umm..."

"Don't worry. I *am* tired. I'll leave you alone as soon as you tell me where you've put the paper and the mail."

"Oh, upstairs on your dresser."

"Good night then." He kissed her sweetly on the cheek. "Don't let the fellow keep you up too late." Then he disappeared and Robbie heard his firm but lingering tread up the stairs. He thought Mairead had a beau in the living room! *There* was irony.... As soon as she heard the door close to his room upstairs, Robbie hauled herself upright and headed for the front door. She didn't like this fugitive sneaking through Christy's own home at all.

Mairead looked agitated as she opened the door. "Ah, Robbie, I'm sorry.... I keep saying it and I *am*."

Robbie patted her head, moved by affection and regret. "It's okay."

For the short walk down dark, leafy Northumberland, Robbie kept her mind blank. Of course Mairead had not meant to cause her pain, but she fervently wished the girl had let things be. She hadn't needed that final glimpse of Christy. It was infinitely more wrenching than seeing Simon again.

But then again, the prospect of seeing Simon again was quite unwelcome enough, Robbie discovered when she arrived back at Mrs. Hall's. The old lady had been propping her eyes open all evening in front of the television, waiting for Robbie to come home so she would be sure to see the message right away.

"As sweet and polite as could be. Said he was staying at the Shelbourne and that you should call him whatever hour you came in."

Sweet and polite to old ladies, that sounded like Simon. "Simon Beyer?" Robbie pressed, unwilling to believe it, despite the weight of evidence. "At the Shelbourne Hotel here in *Dublin*?"

Mrs. Hall cast a critical eye toward her, as if she did not like to be doubted. "That's the name, and didn't I get it right? 'A very dear and close old friend' is how he put it. He must be, to stop here to see you on his way from London to New York. You can use the telephone in the parlor, it's private."

"Oh, no," Robbie countered quickly. "I'm in no mood for him tonight."

"He said he'd be waiting up for you though."

"Simon Beyer has never been known to go to bed before four in the morning anyway. It'll be no hardship for him to wait up all night."

"Well, you know best. Good night, dear. Still, he sounded a very charming man."

Robbie didn't return Simon's call until she had achieved the safety of Emerald Studios and Donal's gruff company the next day. Her ex-mentor/ex-suitor was out; the desk clerk took a message. With great luck she and Simon would continue to miss each other until he got bored and left Ireland.

She and Donal went to work on another song. The album was shaping up nicely. Donal's long experience helped her capture Fire Hazard's spontaneity. Too many New York engineers, at least the circle she had met through Simon, relied on overdubbing and special effects, but Donal's feel for live-sounding music matched hers.

The album was the only area where Robbie's luck held firm that day. Emerald's receptionist buzzed her later in the control room and told her she had a call— Simon had finally tracked her down.

"Hello, Simon." She tried to sound cordial but not particularly warm, a hard balance to find.

"Hello, love. Lord, finding you in Ireland has been like the quest for the Holy Grail."

"Why, Simon, I'm flattered by the comparison."

"That Shane character..."

"Shaw. Michael Shaw."

"Whatever—he acted like he'd take the secret of your whereabouts with him to the grave."

"Well, I was taking a break before mixing this album. You know how you have to get your mind off of music."

His voice dropped to an intimate note. "And you don't think *I* could have gotten your mind off of music?"

Robbie ignored his implication as best she could. "Ireland's hardly the place I'd expect to find you, Simon. Why are you here?"

"What's a few hundred miles between friends? Dublin is between London and New York, after all. I heard you were working on some smashing new project and probably pining away in your leisure time playing darts or whatever it is they do for fun over here. I realized it was really absurd for me to wait to see you in New York and talk to you about something that would just put you right on a plane across the Atlantic again."

Robbie's suspicions were confirmed; he was after her for some reason in particular. "You want to tell me what it is?"

"On the phone, love? Really, I think it deserves at least a nice little supper somewhere—this place has a rather adequate restaurant, if you go in for musty crystal and such..."

"I'm really busy, Simon. I won't have time for 'nice little suppers' until I finish this nice little album. Why don't you give me a sneak preview over the phone?"

His petulant sigh brought vivid images of his pouting face to Robbie's mind. "Darling, you never *have* learned the nicer points of business, have you?"

"You mean like turning everything into an entry on an expense account?"

"In a word. Well, if you must be so brisk, my little surprise is this—Gramotech is talking to me about doing a series of promotional EP's for a string of their new acts. Of course it's a gorgeous big project and I immediately realized that you might enjoy working on it with me. Some of the bands are rather your style."

"No, sorry, Simon. I'm pretty much occupied for the rest of the year. You go ahead and have fun with them.

You wanted to get into a new sound anyway, didn't you?"

"Well—" he sounded tense "—the fact of the matter is that Gramotech is quite keen to have you. I talked you up a great deal, you see."

Robbie saw something else, too, though she never would have thought herself cynical enough to imagine such a thing—Simon *needed* her on this Gramotech project. In fact, she got the feeling that he might have *promised* her to Gramotech in order to get the job himself. She found herself strangely saddened by him, a man who had never accepted the fact that his niche in life might change. He had all the talent in the world, he could have turned his hand to anything in the music business—managing, promoting, A & R, anything. But he kept chasing the spotlight, even now that he had to ride upon other people's reputations. "I'm sorry, Simon. Really, I can't take on anything for the time being. Look, thanks for thinking of me, and I'll probably see you when I get back to New York...."

He would not give up so easily. "New York! Darling, you can hardly leave me at the mercy of these Irish restaurants—let's have a social dinner at least before I go."

"Well, tonight's impossible—I'll be working until all hours."

Donal raised his eyebrows but made no remark.

"Tomorrow then," Simon persisted.

"Oh, no, I'm committed to this little party Lawless is throwing."

Impatience finally started to show in his voice, "Can you fit me in the day after that?"

She was losing her nerve; she had never broken off with him in a decisive way. Technically they were still friends. Besides, she owed him too much to *enjoy* being callous. "I don't think so.... I'm really pushing this album, Simon—I wouldn't even go to the party tomorrow if Michael wasn't counting on me—I really should work."

His sigh sounded martyred. "That's the Robbie I know—puritan work ethic and all. I suppose then I *will* next see you in New York." Abruptly he hung up.

Robbie held the phone in a perplexed hand. Could she have escaped him so easily? That was hardly the Simon she knew.

Chapter Ten

In Dublin airport a man sat, oblivious to the turmoil around him. He held a binder of papers and a pen as if he had been stopped in the middle of making notes in order to pin down a thought. He had been that way for a very long while, and the thought he pursued had nothing to do with the neglected binder.

"Mr. O'Laighleis!" a surprised voice exclaimed in his ear. "Aren't you supposed to be on that flight to Frankfurt?"

Christy looked up into the face of an airport attendant. He traveled to Great Britain and the Continent so frequently many of them knew him by name. "I am. Why?"

"They just announced the final boarding call. You'd better hurry along. The next flight is not for hours."

"Thank you. I must have drifted off." Stuffing his papers into an attaché case, he made an immense effort to pull himself together and board the plane. How did he expect to purchase five thousand pounds worth of German-made broadcasting equipment for the government's new youth project—the one *he* had designed and advocated—if he couldn't even remember to get on the plane? The trip should have been a god-sent opportunity to push thoughts of Robbie out of his mind—he adored traveling even though he was always glad to get home. He ought to be elated by the progress he had made with the government. He had friends he could visit outside of Frankfurt, one of them a very charming woman. Why were his spirits so dull?

His deep sigh drew the concerned smile of a stewardess; he made himself wear a more cheerful expression as he settled himself into the seat. It lasted until the wheels lost contact with the runway. When he touched down again in Ireland in two weeks Robbie would no longer be there. She would be safely back in New York where she would be happier. In time she'd see the truth in what he had told her and thank him for leaving her free to enjoy the success that was rightfully hers.

She would never thank him, however, for the unforgivable clumsy way in which he had treated her. It was as if he had suffered a personality transplant. The unwavering, some would say ruthless, man who had the ear of his nation's rulers, became in her presence unable to control his own impulses. He had to reach out to those slender arms and, time and time again, had to drag himself back. If it had been rough on his own nerves, it must have been no pleasure for her, either. At least there would be half a continent between them from now until she left for the United States.

Half a continent and Simon Beyer. In Christy's attaché case lay a music trade paper with a gossip column that never let a celebrity wander into Ireland without comment. It cattily reported, and with spotty accuracy as far as Christy could tell, that notorious partyer and hit producer Simon Beyer had just popped in from London and was showing interest in unnamed Irish bands.

Christy thought otherwise—Beyer was interested in *Robbie*. Their professional association had been common knowledge for years, and it didn't take a great leap of the imagination to envision a romance between them. What man even half alive could be indifferent to Robbie Calderón? And, since reason insisted that she had been the one to walk away from Beyer, not vice versa, the man was obviously in town to woo her back. That would have been Christy's purpose.

Well, fine. That suited him, too. Perhaps Beyer could make Robbie's transition back to her old life easier.

Robbie's guilty conscience made her work the long hours she had given as an excuse not to see Simon. In a way it was better than going home and fretting over how she had treated him that day, how he had treated her in the past, or, worst of all, what kind of a future he might think they could have together. But it also meant she was overtired for the Lawless party. A long afternoon nap and an early bedtime seemed like the promise of heaven, one she had to forgo.

She stared glumly at the contents of her closet. The ivory silk dress would have suited the subdued, elegant evening Michael had told her to expect, but he might begin to think it the only dress she owned. Resigned, she pulled out the black linen she had come to think of as her "Simon" dress and prepared herself to look out of place at the party. Perhaps they'd write it off to New York weirdness.

Michael picked her up himself and drove her to a spectacular residence on what he informed her was Dublin's embassy row.

"Great street to live on if you're loaded," he explained, pointing out the Japanese embassy next door to their destination. "Wonderful police protection."

"I can imagine. This isn't your house by any chance?"

His laugh was so hearty he nearly choked. "Hardly. No, this is actually no one's home—it's the Dublin headquarters of the British corporation that controls Lawless. They have a few offices here, but mostly it's used for parties where they want to impress someone. Here we are."

Robbie hopped out as a uniformed valet opened the door for her, and waited on the cobblestones while Michael handed him the keys. When the A & R man joined her she asked, "Who are they trying to impress tonight?"

Grinning, he tucked her hand into the crook of his arm and replied, "You."

For a good portion of the evening they succeeded. The furnishings and catering combined the best of Europe, the guests—all Lawless employees and media people—charmed her with their friendliness and ready wit. The only cloud on her enjoyment was the thought that any gathering of the music elite in Ireland not primarily for Lawless people would probably include Christy. If she stayed in Ireland she would encounter him again and again.

Very late in the evening when her energy had started to flag, she heard a flurry of activity in the foyer and glanced over in time to see the dapper form of Simon

Beyer. Her heart nearly jumped out of her chest. Who had so misguidedly invited him here? Michael *knew* she didn't care to see him.

"Roberta!" Her name was called in a drawling English accent. Fatalistically, she forced herself to stand still while he and his party made their way over to her. Simon always traveled with an entourage of cronies who had extreme trendiness to distinguish them if nothing else. He also always seemed to choose brunettes, probably to set off his own white-blond curls. She wondered if he would have made her his protégée if she had been fair-haired. Dwelling on such nonsense was stupid and irritating; she forced herself to stop.

Tonight his curls had been moussed into extravagant waves and his smooth face was framed by the ruffles of a frilly cravat—Simon was always in the vanguard of fashion. But, as awesome as she had thought his command of style, she realized he used clothes and attitude to cover up a rather limp, pallid body. The delicate air of mystery she had sensed around him now seemed to be merely poor health.

"Love! You look smashing, as usual!" he effused. As he bent to kiss her cheek he whispered, "A thoroughbred in a barnyard, I daresay. Look at this crowd. Shaw said they were *music* people but there's not a good haircut among them." Aloud he called to his contingent, "People, this is Roberta, my best pupil. Robbie, meet Zondra, Philippe, and Spider...."

She endured the introductions and then mumbled an excuse to slip away. Simon pouted, but let her go with the promise that she'd come back with someone interesting for him to talk to.

She found Michael Shaw in another room carefully out of earshot of her meeting with Simon. He did not appear surprised to see her. "Robbie, darling, having a good time?"

"Oh, come on, Michael, don't act the innocent."

He lifted a brow but couldn't keep his eyes from straying toward the sound of Simon's supercilious laughter.

"Aha! It *was* you that invited him!" she declared accusingly.

"Why, I thought you might be getting tired of us and our fusty old ways. I thought perhaps a visit from an old friend might—"

She interrupted impatiently. "Might remind me of just how much higher the social life in Ireland rates over New York?"

He avoided her eyes and shifted uncomfortably. "Umm...there might have been a wee bit of that in my motive. Did it work?"

She shook her head, regretting the lie. How could she explain to him that the problem was not Ireland's *lack* of attractions but its *wealth* of them—one in particular?

"I'm sorry, Robbie."

"You can make it up to me."

"How?" He beamed in fresh hope.

"Sneak me out a side door and take me home. I'm about to practice a little New York rudeness."

Simon Beyer left town without a further assault and only Robbie's guilty conscience was left to bother her. The test pressings arrived from London and she arranged one final stint in the studio for the listening. Success! The lab had caught all the lively ambience of the tape with little distortion. She approved the masters and indulged in a round of toasts and kisses with Donal and the technicians.

Donal, one Guinness away from being incoherent, broke his usual dry reserve to mourn the end of Robbie's work at Emerald. "Ah, girl, it's a great shame you're not happy enough with us here to stay on. I'm not one to blow me own horn, but what do those New York studios have that we don't?"

"Arrogant jerks," Robbie replied promptly, then, astonished, took note of what she had said. She had never allowed herself to see that even her accustomed sanctum—the studio—was not free from intrusions, but it was true. Every session she had ever worked had been plagued from time to time by obnoxious record executives or offensive friends of those executives or the artists or the manager. Every session but this one at Emerald. "How can I really work without shallow, pompous, bossy VIP's telling me what to do and causing hysteria? Really, Donal, do you want to spoil me?"

He gazed at her wisely, or perhaps it was just drunkenly. "Who's to say you're not spoiled already? You've lived *here* now, how *can* you go back? Where's that Michael Shaw fellow when you need him anyway? He should be keeping you here." He staggered off to call Michael on the telephone, oblivious to the fact that it was four o'clock on a Saturday afternoon and even a go-getter like Michael would be taking a little time off for himself. Fortunately an untended bottle of porter distracted him and he never reached the phone.

Michael, however, *was* on the job. He turned up later laden with flowers, champagne, his wife's homemade soda bread and a firm contract offer from Lawless's management. "I mean it, Robbie you won't do better in America or Britain—a nice expense account to scout new bands, a great deal of freedom in signing them, final say on recording studios, input on cover art, promotion.... You've got to admit we're practically giving you a company of your own."

"I know," she agreed, somewhat dazed at the opportunity before her—an opportunity she could not take.

Michael continued softly, "And it's not a bad little country, is it?"

"No, it isn't.... She was beginning to feel unsteady; she wished he would just take a simple "no" and not pry. Everything he said was true, but one fact rendered all the advantages inadequate—staying in Ireland would bring her in constant contact with Christy.

"And I think the way we do things here suits you."

"Michael, please. I *do* have my reasons." He must have deduced from the desperate edge to her voice that it was time to shut up. He breathed a resigned sigh. "Just consider that the offer is always open. If you get to New York and change your mind you can hop right back on another plane. Heck, if you change your mind at thirty-five thousand feet you can get the plane to *turn around*."

She giggled a little. "Thanks, I'll tell the pilot you said that."

It seemed that she would manage to leave Ireland without one last traumatic glimpse of Christy. Mairead and the band threw her a dinner in Howth at which they unveiled the artwork for the album and got very drunk on wine and maudlin goodbyes. Afterward she and Mairead slouched in front of the big fieldstone fireplace, planning Fire Hazard's first visit to America.

"You'll take me to all the clubs and introduce me to every big rock star you know. I have to start finding out if they really *will* bore me. And all your friends, too—at least *they* are bound to be interesting."

"Oh, I don't know about that...."

Mairead poked her. "Well, of course they are, silly. Why else would you be friends with them?"

"I have no idea."

Mairead shook her head like a dog shaking water out of its ears. "I must be totally soused, that doesn't make sense. But I'm sure no amount of explaining will get through to me. What time is your plane tomorrow?"

"Eight in the evening."

"Oh, then we've got lots of time to be serious about saying goodbye. As for now—I'm off to bed."

Unsteadily they helped each other up the stairs. Mairead fell across her bed and into a deep sleep immediately. Robbie, again in Rose's room, had a harder time finding comfort under the quilts. She listened half-consciously for noises next door from Christy's old room and tried not to feel sorry for herself. It was almost better to let her mind actively dread the return to New York—when she managed to empty it the very first unguarded thoughts that crept in were sensations of Christy—how his rough cheek had felt on her breasts, how his weight on her had seemed such a comfort. Against her will she imagined his voice in her ear whispering things he had never said, but that she had seen in his eyes. As she lay alone in the dark, she could make him seem so *real*.

Robbie didn't know which of them looked worse the next morning—she from her troubled sleep or Mairead from her hangover. Mrs. Lawless supplied them with endless coffee and sympathetic silence.

"Tell me again, what time does your plane leave?" Mairead moaned.

"Eight tonight."

"Oh, yeah. I'll have to write it down somewhere." The blonde lapsed into wordless suffering.

Robbie found herself staring across the glassy gray sea toward Ireland's Eye. It looked lonely and desolate, exactly the way she felt. She remembered that Christy had said he used to sit there among the gulls and look back at Ireland with a new, remote perspective. That was what she needed—remoteness, something to sever her emotions from this land before she had to physically leave it.

"How does one get out to that little island?"

Mairead wrinkled her nose and squeezed her eyes shut against the sparkle of the sea. "One—by which I suppose you mean *you*—goes down to the harbor and hangs about with a pound note fluttering from her hand. Some old salt will show up with a launch about as sturdy as a paper hat and take you over. Is that what you want to do on your last day in Ireland?"

"Sounds weird, huh? It just suddenly struck me. Would I have time?"

"Oh, aye, we needn't leave for the airport until half past five. No hurry."

"Good, then I'll go play Christopher Columbus and let you sleep off your hangover so you can live through the drive to the airport."

Mrs. Lawless, who had overheard Robbie's plans, pressed a picnic lunch and an afghan into her hands. "If you go home to New York with pneumonia, what'll it do to your memories of Ireland, I ask you?"

Robbie smiled her thanks and kept her mouth shut. Her memories would be difficult enough; pneumonia could hardly make them worse.

Christy applied the brakes harshly and caused the red car to skid across the sandy driveway of his parents' house. What was his rush? Robbie was either still there or she was gone. Mrs. Hall hadn't known the time of her flight, only that she'd be in Howth until then. Christy had abandoned the idea of calling, even if it might be the only way to catch her. His behavior over the past two months had made him seem like a maniac even to himself. Why should Robbie believe anything that came out of his mouth?''

It amazed him to think of how erratic he had been. The only sure, steady value in his life had been his attraction to Robbie...obsession with...oh, call it by its name, he ordered himself—*love.* Falling in love with her had not been the neatest move in his life's plan, but now that it had been accomplished, everything else had to be rethought and jostled to fit. Perhaps it was divine justice; he had approached life with truly awesome arrogance, first in thinking he could alter the course of music with his company, then in thinking he could alter the course of *youth* itself with his grand plan for Irish culture. He had been very quick to make judgements and very severe: British and American influences were ruining the integrity of his homeland, sapping the vitality of its culture. He would somehow single-handedly stem the tide. Except that he had fallen in love with the very personification of American influence and she hadn't an ounce of harm in her lovely, welcoming body.

And still he had assumed he could cast her off as he had rock music. Arrogance! He had never cast off his love for rock. Now here he was driving too fast in order to keep her dear American influence with him in Ireland.

Christy slammed through the front door. "Ma! Mairead!" His voice echoed through the quiet house. Where was everybody? Had they already left for the airport?

Then a thin, irritated reply drifted down from the upstairs, "Oh, don't bellow so, you'll break me poor head in two."

Christy bounded up the stairs and found his sister deep in the shadows of her darkened bedroom. "Has she left yet?"

"By 'she,' do I take it you mean my friend, Robbie?"

"Whoever else would I mean? Is she here?"

"She is and she isn't."

"Mairead!" He imbued his voice with brotherly warning.

She glared indignantly. "I'm surprised you care. You've done enough to drive the poor girl away. Aha! I see by your guilty look that I'm not half wrong. What did you do to her that she won't stay here and marry you—you *did* ask her, didn't you?"

He groaned. "I did not." Sheer reflex saved him from the ashtray that whizzed past his head. "If you're so keen to have Robbie as a sister-in-law, don't you think you'd better have a living brother to marry her to? And perhaps you could tell the same sorry creature *where she is*!"

"Ach, she's out on the island. Paddy Linn took her in his launch."

"So she can spend her last remaining hours in Ireland bailing for dear life? Good work, Lalor."

"So go rescue her, you bum!"

Christy spared Mairead any retort; he had already started for his car and Howth Harbor. With Robbie on the island there was no need to hurry as if he might miss her; still his sense of haste did not abate. He had to find her quickly if only because he could no longer stand feeling so stupid.

He parked across two spaces at the harbor, pulled Paddy Linn out of a pub, away from the pitcher of stout he had bought with Robbie's pound note, and sat in the bow of the decrepit boat, ignoring the old man's evil looks. The rickety vessel putted through the green swells and inched around to the seaward side of the island. Grumbling, Paddy held the boat still as Christy clambered up the steep, seaweed-slicked path.

The island was a generally mild piece of geology, but it had its share of treacherous spots. What if Robbie had tumbled down the cliff face? What if she had broken her leg on one of the fern-ridden paths? With any luck she had stuck to the scallop of dark beach that offered a view of the mainland. Christy climbed past the old watchtower to survey the strand.

She had not stuck to the beach. Judging by the lack of footprints on the smooth, gray sand, she had not even wandered across it. He paused to get a grip on his mounting sense of panic. Small as the island was, it would take hours to search it thoroughly—better to use his brain for once. Where would Robbie be most likely to go?

The top, where else?

Robbie checked her watch—three-thirty. Four and a half hours until her fate would be sealed. How many times could she run the same cycle of useless thoughts through her brain between now and then? She couldn't see herself getting on that plane. She could see herself at Mrs. Hall's, in Emerald Studios, in Michael Shaw's office, but not on that plane, and most particularly, not in New York. Yet she had to go back. What in the world would she do in Ireland?

That was where the most useless part of the cycle began. She had somehow, unmonitored, deep in her subconscious, developed a last-ditch plan to present to Michael—a deal that would enable her to sign the Lawless contract with a clear conscience. If Lawless wanted to give her freedom to scout and sign acts, she'd use it to find truly *Irish* bands, whatever that meant. She'd pick up where Christy had left off and turn at least part of his old company back to its original purpose. The neatness of the plan pleased her.

Its absurdity didn't. She knew deep down that this stunningly just plan covered a selfish desire to make herself acceptable to the founder of Lawless Records. This was as juvenile and blind a hope as she had ever nurtured. Christy was no idiot, he could see and think as well as she. If he had thought that such a solution might work, or if he had *wanted* it to work, he could have made the suggestion himself. If she stayed in Ireland on premises as shaky as those she was contemplating, she'd tumble right off into the cold Irish Sea. If Christy had *wanted* her, he would have *asked* for her.

So, as inconceivable as it might seem, she would get on that plane.... After she spent a few moments in a dulled void, the cycle would begin again. What would Michael Shaw say if...

Then, during one round of self-torture, as if her thoughts of Christy were so strong they conjured up his presence, she felt the need to turn around. There he stood on the rocks. The wind had thrown his beautiful, wheaten hair into a chaos that matched the reckless emotion in his eyes. The wild vitality that had always surged beneath his urbane surface harmonized with the vigor of the land. He had never lost whatever elusive element made him unique from all the other men she had ever met, whether the ingredient was a product of conscious will or something he had absorbed from the air of his homeland. The force of his stare and the unexpectedness of his presence drove coherent thought from her mind. All she could do was to voicelessly say his name.

It was enough. In one driven movement he crossed the lichen-covered rock and dropped to his knees before her. He leaned forward, drawn to a wire's tension by urgency, yet not daring to touch even so much as the fringe of the afghan around her. His low, fervent voice undercut the whisper of the wind. "I've no right to ask you this—I've certainly done nothing to make you believe I have an ounce of sanity in my head, the way I've knocked you back and forth and the great patriotic speeches I've made at you—I know I must seem the most faithless man in Ireland but I have to ask you anyway..."

Frustration gave her back control of her tongue. "Ask me what?"

"Not to go."

This reduced Robbie to a noise of surprise.

As she scrambled after her spinning thoughts, Christy shook his head and held up one hand. "Please listen awhile. I'd never pretend that Dublin could replace New

York or London, but it wouldn't need to. You could think of it as your home in the suburbs, you see. A nice quiet place to come back to whenever you could or whenever you felt the need.''

Confused, she began uncertainly. "You're not talking about the contract with Lawless, are you?"

He gestured an emphatic "no" with his entire eloquent body. "Heavens, no—I know it's not enough for you, I've known that all along—and I've *said* it, even if I've been muddled about the rest. No, I'd never want to bury you here among the blackberry bushes, no matter how well they suit me."

"Then, Christy, what are we talking about? If you didn't come as an advocate for Lawless, why *did* you come?"

He flushed and Robbie felt warmth spread through her. "Oh, didn't I say then?"

"No!"

He sat back on his heels and stared at the ground, his brave shoulders bracing him to reveal the purpose of his trip. "I thought perhaps that you might consent to marry me."

As she sat in stunned silence he looked up; his eyes were so hurt and his face so wan with desolation she knew he was beginning to interpret her silence as refusal. To gain some time while she adjusted, she said, "I thought you said you didn't want me just on weekends or whenever I could get away."

"I was wrong—I'll take whatever you can give me and thank God in heaven for every minute. Robbie darling, when I was stepping onto that plane from Germany this morning thinking you might have already left for New York, I had no heart to come home. I was always safe loving Ireland, you see. I could make all my plans and pretend I was lovingly directing her toward some glorious goal of my own proud design. She never talked back, she never said, 'Christy, you're a tomfool idiot.'"

"That doesn't sound so terrible," Robbie commented quietly.

His eyes flickered up and met her with frankness. "But it was. A country is a cold lover. She never criticized me but neither did she say, 'Christy, you're a man,' and then put her arms around me to make me feel the truth of her words."

His entreating face was so close she could smell the salty musk of his skin, could see each of the shadow colors that made up the deep dark of his eyes.

"Will you put your arms around me, Robbie?"

Her arms had already started to reach for him, hungry to wrap themselves around his strength and vulnerability. She breathed into his half-parted lips, "What do you feel now, Christy?"

"Fear," he replied.

"Why?"

"You haven't yet answered me."

She smiled into his worried eyes and kissed him lightly on the tip of his fine nose. "The only fear you should have is that Paddy Linn will climb up here to see what's become of us and will *find* me answering you."

The smile he returned was a glowing dawn of relief and his eyes sparkled. "Then I have no fears at all. I told Paddy to stay away for a couple more hours."

"You could have made me miss my plane!"

"I thought I might need every minute I could scrape together to convince you to marry me."

"Oh dear, now what will you do with all your extra time?"

He gathered her up and pulled her, blanket and all, into his arms. He placed the promise of a kiss on her lips. "I was thinking I could make good on a claim I once made to you."

"What was that?"

"That I was a fairly good teacher."

"Oh yeah, I always wondered about that...."

"And what did you wonder?" he asked with mock sharpness.

"If I would be a good pupil."

"Oh you *will* be." His next kiss was a promise no longer, but the very substance of his life and love.

Silhouette Romance

COMING NEXT MONTH

CHAMPAGNE GIRL—Diana Palmer
Underneath Catherine's bubbly facade, there was much more to
the champagne girl. But could she leave Matt and her home in
Texas for a job in the bright city lights of New York?

LAUGHTER IN THE RAIN—Debbie Macomber
Although Abby loved Logan, she would still dream about
storybook romance. Tate seemed to walk right out of the pages—
but how long can you hold on to a dream?

THE PAINTED VEIL—Elizabeth Hunter
Thirsa hid her emotions behind her painting. It brought great
artistic success...but left little room for romance. Until
Luis Kirkpatrick. The painter could see her soul—and share her
deepest desires.

HERO IN BLUE—Terri McGraw
Tara was an attorney fighting her first case as public defender.
She was determined not to mix business with pleasure, but
Lieutenant Dan DeAngelo was putting her heart under arrest.

GETTING PHYSICAL—Marie Nicole
Rory had to compete in a minitriathlon to inherit her late uncle's
physical fitness empire. Zak was thrilled to help her train—and
show her the fitness of getting physical...with him!

SWEET MOCKINGBIRD'S CALL—Emilie Richards
More romance among the MacDonald clan, that fun-loving
family you read about in *Sweet Georgia Gal*. Find out what
happens to Wendy and Shane...would their childhood love
endure after seven years?

AVAILABLE NOW:

THE INFAMOUS MADAM X
Joan Smith

LOOKALIKE LOVE
Nancy John

IRISH EYES
Lynnette Morland

DARLING DETECTIVE
Karen Young

TALL, DARK AND HANDSOME
Glenda Sands

STOLEN PROMISE
Christine Flynn

AMERICAN TRIBUTE

Where a man's dreams count
for more than his parentage...

*Look for these upcoming titles
under the Special Edition
American Tribute banner.*

CHEROKEE FIRE
Gena Dalton #307–May 1986
It was Sabrina Dante's silver spoon that
Cherokee cowboy Jarod Redfeather couldn't
trust. The two lovers came from opposite
worlds, but Jarod's Indian heritage taught
them to overcome their differences.

NOBODY'S FOOL
Renee Roszel #313–June 1986
Everyone bet that Martin Dante and Cara
Torrence would get together. But Martin
wasn't putting any money down, and Cara
was out to prove that she was nobody's fool.

MISTY MORNINGS, MAGIC NIGHTS
Ada Steward #319–July 1986
The last thing Carole Stockton wanted was to
fall in love with another politician, especially
Donnelly Wakefield. But under a blanket of
secrecy, far from the campaign spotlights,
their love became a powerful force.

AM-TRIB-1R

AMERICAN
TRIBUTE

*American Tribute titles
now available:*

RIGHT BEHIND THE RAIN
Elaine Camp #301—April 1986
The difficulty of coping with her brother's
death brought reporter Raleigh Torrence
to the office of Evan Younger, a police
psychologist. He helped her to deal with
her feelings and emotions, including love.

THIS LONG WINTER PAST
Jeanne Stephens #295—March 1986
Detective Cody Wakefield checked out
Assistant District Attorney Liann McDowell,
but only in his leisure time. For it was the
danger of Cody's job that caused Liann to
shy away.

LOVE'S HAUNTING REFRAIN
Ada Steward #289—February 1986
For thirty years a deep dark secret kept them
apart—King Stockton made his millions while
his wife, Amelia, held everything together.
Now could they tell their secret, could they
admit their love?

OFFICIAL SWEEPSTAKES INFORMATION

PURCHASE NECESSARY. To enter, complete the official entry/ order form. Be sure to indicate whether or not you wish to take advantage of our subscription offer.

2. Entry blanks have been pre-selected for the prizes offered. Your response will be checked to see if you are a winner. In the event that these are not claimed, a random drawing will be held from all entries received to award not less than $150,000 in prizes. This is in addition to any free, surprise or mystery gifts which might be offered. Versions of this sweepstakes with different prizes will appear in Torstar Ltd. mailings and their affiliates. Winners selected will receive the prize offered in their sweepstakes insert.

3. This promotion is being conducted under the supervision of Marden-Kane, an independent judging organization. By entering the sweepstakes, each entrant accepts and agrees to be bound by these rules and the decisions of the judges which shall be final and binding. Odds of winning in the random drawing are dependent upon the total number of entries received. Taxes, if any, are the sole responsibility of the prize winners. Prizes are non-transferable. All entries must be received by August 31, 1986.

4. This sweepstakes package offers:

1, Grand Prize :	Cruise around the world on the QEII	$100,000 total value
4, First Prizes :	Set of matching pearl necklace and earrings	$ 20,000 total value
10, Second Prizes:	Romantic Weekend in Bermuda	$ 15,000 total value
25, Third Prizes :	Designer Luggage	$ 10,000 total value
200, Fourth Prizes :	$25 Gift Certificate	$ 5,000 total value
		$150,000

Winners may elect to receive the cash equivalent for the prizes offered.

5. This offer is open to residents of the U.S. and Canada, 18 years and older, except employees of Torstar Ltd., its affiliates, subsidiaries, Marden-Kane and all other agencies and persons connected with conducting this sweepstakes. All Federal, State and local laws apply. Void in the province of Quebec and wherever prohibited or restricted by law. Winners will be notified by mail and may be required to execute an affidavit of eligibility and release which must be returned within 14 days after notification. Canadian winners will be required to answer a skill testing question. Winners consent to the use of their names, photograph and/or likeness for advertising and publicity purposes in conjunction with this and similar promotions without additional compensation. One prize per family or household.

6. For a list of our most current prize winners, send a stamped, self-addressed envelope to: WINNERS LIST, c/o Marden-Kane, P.O. Box 19404, Long Island City, New York 11101.

SSR-A-1